Cathie Dunsford is director of Dunsford Publishing Consultants which has brought 120 new authors into print in the Pacific. She has taught writing, literature and publishing at Auckland University since 1975 in the English Department and through Continuing Education, and was Fulbright Post-Doctoral Scholar at the University of California Berkeley 1983–6. She has co-directed three national writers' conferences, and her work has been published in the USA, Canada, the UK, Australia, New Zealand and in translation in Germany. Her writing has achieved wide acclaim and she is recipient of the Scholarship in Letters and the Established Writers Grant from CNZ Arts Council. She recently completed a book tour of Germany. Cath Dunsford believes readers are vital to the life of an author and welcomes your feedback: <dunsford@voyager.co.nz>.

Other books by Cathie Dunsford

Fiction
Cowrie
The Journey Home: Te Haerenga Kainga
Kia Kaha Cowrie (Rogner & Bernhard, Germany)

Poetry
Survivors: Uberlebende

Anthologies
New Women's Fiction
The Exploding Frangipani (with Susan Hawthorne)
Subversive Acts
Me and Marilyn Monroe
Car Maintenance, Explosives and Love
(with Susan Hawthorne and Susan Sayer)

MANAWA TOA
Heart Warrior

Cathie Dunsford

Spinifex Press Pty Ltd
504 Queensberry Street
North Melbourne, Vic. 3051
Australia
women@spinifexpress.com.au
http://www.spinifexpress.com.au

First published by Spinifex Press, 2000
Copyright © Text: Cathie Dunsford, 2000
Copyright © Typesetting and layout: Spinifex Press Pty Ltd, 2000
Copyright © Woodcut designs: Cathie Dunsford,
Starfish Enterprise Art, New Zealand 2000

Edited by Janet Mackenzie
Typeset in Sabon by Palmer Higgs Pty Ltd
Cover design by Deb Snibson, based on woodcut design
by Cathie Dunsford

Made and printed in Australia by Australian Print Group

National Library of Australia
Cataloguing-in-Publication data:
Dunsford Cathie
   Manawa Toa/Heart Warrior
   ISBN 1 875559 69 8.
I. Title.

A823.3

*Manawa Toa: Heart Warrior is dedicated to all
Maohi and Pacific Islanders.*

*Manawa Toa is a taonga or gift for all those
struggling for a better world.*

Let us have a nuclear free Pacific, a nuclear free world.

Acknowledgements

Creative New Zealand for providing an established writer's arts council grant enabling the time to work on this novel. Rosemary Wildblood for her support for Aotearoan writers.

Susan, Renate, Nikki and all at Spinifex Press for their acknowledgement of the importance of Pacific talkstory in all its forms and their ongoing commitment to publishing Pacific authors globally, and Susan Hawthorne for astute editorial advice.

Beryl Fletcher, Susan Sayer and Karin Meissenburg for comments at draft stages.

Zohl de Ishtar for her honouring of Pacific talkstory on colonial and anti-nuclear themes in *Daughters of the Pacific* (Spinifex Press).

Dr Timoti Karetu for providing sources for checking origins of Maori proverbs and for his support for te reo Maori in Aotearoa.

Witi Ihimaera for his continuing support for my writing and aroha. Kia ora, Witi—yes, "the kaupapa sees us through".

Keri Hulme for always being there and providing support in the tough writing times.

To all my whanau, kia ora, mahalo, thanks for your support.

Rogner and Bernhard, Hamburg, for buying Cowrie series rights from Spinifex at the Frankfurt Bookfair, thereby bringing South Pacific talkstory into the northern hemisphere in translation, and for their excellent editorial advice; Dr Karin Meissenburg for her sensitive translation of *Kia Kaha Cowrie* and her support.

Dr Terry Carlbom, PEN International Secretary, for his enthusiastic support for *Cowrie* at a crucial stage of the writing. Tena koe, Terry.

Sara Fuller, Ginette Pernet, Carolyn Gammon, and other overseas readers and reviewers for their abilities to stretch beyond European boundaries to enjoy Pacific talkstory.

Maohi and Maori tangata whenua who contributed stories and tales of the effects of nuclear testing in the Pacific. *Ehara taku toa i te toa takitahi engari te toa takatini.*

Excerpts from *Manawa Toa, Heart Warrior* have been published in: *Hecate, Bamboo Ridge, Hawai'i Writer's Review, Calyx, Car Maintenance, Explosives and Love* and the Australian Women's Book Review. Thanks to all editors for their support of my work.

Tama tu, tama ora, tama moe, tama mate.
The person who stands, lives; the person who sleeps,
dies.

*The moon guides a canoe over silent black water, then
disappears. Frogmen in an inflatable boat zoom towards
figures waiting on the sand. As they reach the shore, the
moon slides from its eclipse to the sound of helicopter
blades and gunshots. They dive for cover, some into the
water, some to the bottom of the craft. She watches from
the beach. A bullet tears past her leg. She plunges into the
ocean, her fins stretching to power her toward the craft.
Waves lash her face. Her shell protects her back from
bullets shooting through the water. She draws in a huge
breath and dives as deep as she can. Beneath the surface,
it is black. Seaweed tangles in her fins. She struggles to
fight free.*

Cowrie wakes. The moon edges her way over the
dunes and shines through the trunks of her nikau palm
hut. She cannot get back to sleep. She wraps her lavalava
around her large, strong body and walks across the
dunes to the ocean. Stalks of marram grass lit by moonlight remind her of Peta's sweetgrass. As she reaches the
last dune, the wild West Coast wind lashes at her face,
fills her lungs. She draws in a deep breath, remembers the
nightmare. *He titi rere ao, ka kitea; he titi rere po, e kore
e kitea.**

---

*Welcome visitors arrive by day; night visitors are enemies who come
in the dark. (Literally: A muttonbird which flies by day is seen; the
bird which flies by night is unseen.)

A lone torea plunges its beak into the sand to dredge up a tuatua which spits in the bird's face as it is raised from its sleepy depths. The torea flies away, leaving the tuatua to burrow its way back to freedom. Moonlight catches the white water as waves break far out at sea. Brilliant stars sparkle over the Pacific shores. She imagines navigating her way through these breakers in the dark. Ancestral waka came from all over the Pacific guided only by stars. There were no stars in her dream, just a blanket of blackness covering them until the whirring and gunshots, then a glaring light. She recalls Keo telling her Mika's story about finding the Hawai'ian fishermen, Aka and Vile, shot in the moonlight as they tried to escape from the enemy. It's said they had entered into the American nuclear testing zone and were pursued back to Ka Lae. Aka was shot scaling the cliff face and found dangling in the fisherman's ropes. Vile was blasted in his back as he secured the canoe. Maybe this was the source of her dream? No-one knew for sure what had happened but speculation led to the US military.

Cowrie shivers, the night wind tugging her lavalava. She walks up the beach to the driftwood log in the shape of a stranded whale, the place that marks her rescue of little Maata from drowning. It's good to be back in Aotearoa, where threats are from the wildness of nature and the pull of waves rather than gunshots piercing the darkness.

Ko Uenuku tawhana i te rangi.
Uenuku, the God of Rainbows, like a bow in the sky.

"Oho, Cowrie! Wake up!" Mere's voice cuts into her sleep. Drowsily, she opens her eyes. "It's after ten. You're s'posed to be at kohanga reo. Shift your lazy bum and get up there!" Her mother throws her lavalava over to the mattress and exits the opening of the nikau hut.

Still dazed by her sleepless night, Cowrie wraps the purple and yellow hibiscus cloth around her body and ambles to the kohanga. The children laugh at her tousled hair and know she has just risen. They tease her relentlessly. To divert their attention, she tempts them with a story if they gather round her feet. Kids in all shapes and sizes fall about her like waves swirling around seaweed in the ocean.

Once they are all settled and she's wiped a few snotty noses, she asks them who's ever seen a dolphin? Of course, most of them have and all of them know the famous story of Opo, the gay dolphin who haunted the shores of nearby Opononi, on the inner Hokianga harbour, in the fifties. Their parents have told them tales of the magic fish that graced their beaches for years until one day it was lured away by a fisherman and found stranded in a rock pool, unable to escape.

"Now I'll tell you a different dolphin tale. This one is a Chumash story."

"What's Shoe-mush, Cowrie?"

3

"Chumash is the name of a Native American tribe—an iwi like Nga Puhi, who lived on the west coast of the Pacific Ocean, on the shell of Great Turtle Island."

"What's Great Turtle Island?" pipes up a Yugoslav kid, descended from the early gumdiggers in the area.

"That's America, silly," asserts Maata, proud of her knowledge.

"Shoosh," say the others, keen to hear the rest of the story.

Cowrie lowers her voice to keep their attention. "The Chumash people thrived so well they could no longer live on the island of Santa Cruz, so Hutash dreamed into life a rainbow bridge to carry them across to Carpinteria on the mainland."

"Is mainland the back of the turtle?" asks Matiu.

"Course it is," chips in Maata.

"Shoosh" comes the chorus, allowing Cowrie to continue.

Like all storytellers, she elaborates on the story each time she tells it. She gets the kids to identify the colours of the rainbow and they listen carefully as she explains how the rainbow bridge is created and then how, when people fell off it during the crossing, they were turned into dolphins and set free into the wide ocean. How dolphins came to be sacred to the tribe because they knew that some of these creatures were their aunties and uncles and cousins and sisters.

"How did the aunties get inside? Did the dolphins eat them?"

"No. They became dolphins when they entered the water. So they could be free." Cowrie thinks of the transformation of Peta, her return to Kahnawake, to Nanduye, her need to reconnect with her people through their work together.

4

"So, was Opo one of our ancestors?" asks Hone.

"May well have been," replies Cowrie. She's never thought of this before. Strange how kids so often get right to the core of the truth. It's as if they have some knowledge buried deep in them.

"Did Opo come back to tell us something?" asks Maata.

Cowrie has to think a moment. "Perhaps so, Maata. When Opo first came, everyone was touched by her dolphin spirit, her friendliness with people. She'd swim close to the shore, even touching people with her fins. But later, when greedy men tried to cash in on the act, the dolphin was harassed by people throwing their kids on her back, by crowds of tourists entering the water and trying to touch her. Instead of appreciating her, they wanted to possess her, own her, have a piece of her."

"Is that why she disappeared?"

"It's said she followed a fisherman up the harbour and her sonar was disturbed by blasting in the water, but she could also have been exhausted from the attention and people not leaving her alone."

"So we killed her then," asserts Marama.

"One way or the other, yes," Cowrie replies.

"Did she come to warn us about greed?"

"I think so. She came for many reasons. Maybe she was once one of us. But she serves as a lesson that we still need to learn."

"I'd like to be turned into a dolphin. I could swim anywhere I wanted and if too many people hassled me, I'd just swim back out to the open sea," asserts Piripi.

"Right on, Piripi. Now, I want you all to draw the story of Hutash and the rainbow bridge or Opo or anything we've talked about this morning."

The children gather their crayons and lay large sheets of newsprint from the *Hokianga Herald* on the floor. Tongues out, green, blue, orange, yellow crayons grasped as if they are a lifeline to the spirit. Cowrie can't resist a smile as she sees uncles, aunties and brothers being turned into strange dolphin-like creatures and coloured arcs bursting from islands into the skies and falling gently on the land beyond. One picture depicts a rainbow stretching from the shores of Opononi over to the dunes and a dolphin splashing out of the water, stars bursting around its body.

"Why the stars, Hone?"

"They're tear drops. They dazzle in the water then turn into tiny dolphins. They live in the wreck of the *Rainbow Warrior*. I know 'cos my dad took me out there last summer and dived down into the sunken boat. He said there were fish living all over it."

Cowrie is close to tears herself. "Ae, Hone. Out of death, new life."

"But the French still shouldn't have sunk her with that bomb, eh Cowrie?"

"No, Maata. No they shouldn't."

"I'm gonna walk the rainbow bridge and fall into the water and turn into a dolphin so I can protect all the protest ships at sea so we can stay a clean, green land," states Maata. The kids get excited and all agree it'd be a good life underwater. Bright colours erupt from their canvases, fill the room with hope, shimmering out the windows like a rainbow arc emerging from the misty water when the sun shines through.

*He korero taua ki Wharaurangi, he korero ta matau
ki Otuawhaki.*
The talk is of war at Wharaurangi, but at
Otuawhaki, they speak of making fishhooks.

Kuini pokes her head through the entrance to Cowrie's
hut. "Kia ora, sis. You still hard at it? Time for a break,
I reckon."

"You can talk! I've seen your candlelight flicker-
ing in Tainui past midnight for the last three weeks!
I nearly came in one night when I had a bad nightmare
and couldn't get back to sleep. But just as I approached,
you must've blown the candle out so I strolled to the
beach."

"I guess we've both been hard at it. But I've finished
the draft proposals for establishing Te Aroha abuse
prevention scheme nationally and I'm ready for some
relaxation.Wanna go fishin'?"

"Aw, dunno, Kuini. Still got heaps of work to do."

"I thought you'd given up that bloody thesis stuff."

"Have. But writing for a feminist press is as hard,
only I don't have to fight the academy to be heard now.
The same amount of research has to be done."

"Virtual reality hits the Hokianga! If Dale Spender is
right, you'll be forgetting about the printed page anyhow.
Books'll cost too much, deplete the rainforest, but
electronic media will be an eighth of the price and more
accessible."

"Yeah, and useful for political action. Koana has been
emailing progress on land disputes on the Big Island."

"So you'll be ready for some kai moana then, eh?"

Cowrie sighs, knowing she's had the best out of the day and her mind is too tired to be of much value in the remaining hours. "You're on. You get the paddles and kayaks ready and I'll bring the fishing gear."

Kuini needs no encouraging. She's off to the beach in a flash to unhitch the kayaks from the pohutukawa trees and pull up the paddles from under the ferns. In the shed behind Mere's cottage, Cowrie unfurls the lines from the last expedition, pissed off that someone has used them without cutting the bait from the hooks. It stinks. The marae cats could've had a nasty experience. As she saunters over the dunes, she feels the sun on her face and a weight lift from her shoulders.

The wahine pull the spray skirts for the kayaks tight around their bodies so that they can get through the huge breakers without swamping their craft. This also allows them to spin into an eskimo roll and do a 360-degree turn to paddling position if they are swamped by a wave. Water swirls around their legs as they prepare the kayaks for take-off. It's crucial to time the waves perfectly or you can get dunked before you've got up a decent paddling speed. Kuini yells "E oma!" and they use their paddles to shove off from the beach, stroking for their lives to make it through the breakers.

As the first wave towers over them and crashes down onto the canoes, Cowrie lets out a shout of joy, emerging from the water cascading over her as her waka springs back to the surface. Kuini begins a mad haka, yelling at the waves in time with the beat of her paddle, and each races to be first to get beyond the breakers. At each cry of "te waka" they hit a wave and skim neatly through its curled cave. Ten minutes and several eskimo rolls later, they are both beyond the breaking surf, triumphant. No matter how often they do this, it always captures the excitement of the first time. West Coast breakers are renowned for their power and many trawlers and old sailing ships from England never made it past the Hokianga sand bar, their wrecks emerging from the surf at low tide as testament to their ghostly journeys.

Paddling beyond the breakers, they follow the flight of torea, akiaki and takapu. Giant gannets dive down into the ocean swooping up fish in their beaks. Ahead of them, a school of kahawai leap from the water, thrashing about on the surface trying to escape the beaks of the gulls. Mollymawks and takapu cruise on the wind currents, waiting for the exact moment to skim the surface and pluck a rich treat of kai moana from the sea. The wahine paddle into the centre of the thrashing fish, dragging their lines behind the kayaks. Within seconds, ika are pulling at the bait. Every line has six hooks on it and they wait until they have a few tails crashing from the wake before they reel in their catches. Each fish is gently taken from the paua and bone hooks and killed immediately with a prick to its head. Soon, the kete at their feet are so full they have to chuck one in the front and one in the back to balance the kayaks for the journey home.

They stroke out parallel with the shore, the sun lowering into the far ocean to starboard. As it sinks, a bright orange glow lights the sky, reflecting off the clouds. Taniwha fly into the horizon, seahorses, feather starfish, crawling octopuses, flying ika change shape as the clouds move and rearrange themselves. They surf in on the waves, the horizon behind them lit with that haunting pounamu shade which signifies an Aotearoan West Coast sunset.

From: koana@hilo.com
To: turtle@hokianga.co.nz

Aloha Cowrie,

How are you, Turtle? Have been thinking of you lately.
Just returned from a week-long Kanaka Maoli gathering.
We discussed land sovereignty issues and there were a
range of related workshops. Pele Aloha talked about the
importance of retaining the ancient art of talkstory which
some of our younger ones are losing. You'd have loved it.
We've decided to make this an important initiative for the
upcoming Nuclear Free and Independent Pacific Conference.
It's crucial that haole have our input to this from our
perspective.

I'm excited by the work, but the small actions we each take
sometimes seem so minimal. Do you ever feel swamped by
the hugeness of the task? Ela and I believe that every small
action counts and we teach our kids that too. Nele and Peni
are becoming more involved in Kanaka Maoli activities and
it's exciting to see them reconnecting with the traditions of
our 'ohana—beyond what Ela and I, Meleana and Paneke can
provide for them.

Can you send us information on how to get our work into
print? Community Education at Hilo have provided us free
use of their desktop publishing facilities. But we need to
know of other Pacific presses that we can network with.
We need to know how we can get our work out to a wider
readership.

Mauva emailed from Tahiti Fa'a'a. Tavini Haraatira is getting
stronger. They're sick of the French domination and military

presence. Problem is, so many of the men earn income from it. The islands have become dependent on the colonial power. It's complex. But freedom will come soon. They must get their land back. You know, the same old story through all our islands.

Nele is completing a school project documenting local ki'i pohaku. She's recreated some of the rock drawings on paper and Peni is etching some of them into stones he finds on the beach. They've included some here for you.

Malamo pono, Turtle. I'll hand you over to them.

Hi Cowrie! Peni and I drew these for you on screen and Koana showed us how to transfer them to email. Remember that day we followed the lava trail at Puako? We went back there

on a school trip and showed everyone the magic shapes.
Now we're making up a book of sketches so they will be here
for other kids in the future and for those who cannot get to
the isolated sites. Some of the other kids are pissed 'cos
we get to draw for our project and they have to write
essays—but we reckon it's ok 'cos we thought of it first!

Mahalo for that video you sent of the kohanga kids surfing
down those gigantic sand dunes and into the sea.
Awesome! We took it to school and everyone wanted to see
it over and over. The best part was watching them zoom out
of the ocean and back up the dunes in reverse motion! None
of us have ever seen dunes that huge. Like the Sahara
Desert in the middle of the South Pacific. We can't wait to
visit. Koana says she'll bring us over for the next Nuclear-
Free Pacific conference.

Aloha—Neli and Pene

From: sappho@island.ac.uk
To: turtle@hokianga.co.nz

Dear Cowrie,

Thank you for responding to my letter. I appreciate the
depth of your enquiry. I have had to think hard about
answering all your questions. They came as rather a
surprise. But on further reflection, I see why you've asked
them. I assure you that my motives are pure. The last thing
I want is to appropriate Pacific traditions. My point is to
discover for myself what the issues are and find a way to
get people here to become more involved. As you know, many
Brits still regard New Zealand and Australia as the colonies
where we sent remittance men and convicts. There is a kind
of snobbery that typifies our perceptions about your
countries. Added to this, the rest of the Pacific is seen as
an island paradise provided specifically for Europeans to
have idyllic holidays. The real issues seldom get aired and it
is hard to get through to English people that we are a part
of the problem. As a young British person I feel it is my
responsibility to address these issues and use my own
networks to distribute the information gained.

As to your other enquiries—no, I'm not a part of the
aristocracy! My dad works in the lime quarries near
Ashbourne in Derbyshire and lives in a council flat! He
reckons the royals are parasites living on the backs of the
working class and the Tories have "sold out to the Frogs
and other slimey creatures from Europe!" He's pretty racist
really but he's solidly for the workers. Got his team to go on
strike for weeks over the poll tax. Sees immigrants as
stealing jobs from working Brits. It's a confused world out
there. One I want to be a part of changing.

Yes, I did go to university—Birmingham. Completed a master's in literature, took a journalism course at the Poly. I was an anarchist, ready to burn down the whole bloody Empire! But after Greenham, I saw we could have a lasting effect. I didn't realise how strong women could be. I never got to know my mum, really. My parents split up when I was a kid and she left for France. I've not seen her since. One of my brothers works at the quarry, one is unemployed. I'm closest to Crispin, the eldest, who is a naturalist working in Antarctica. He and I were the only ones who went to university because we got scholarships that paid the fees.

Anyway, enough about me. Do I get to ask you questions too? How come you left the Fulbright at UC Berkeley and what brought you back to Te Kotuku Marae? What are you doing there now? Can I come and visit you and discuss the project in more depth? The British anti-nuclear group I belong to have suggested I do a series of articles and will sponsor me for part of the costs. The rest I'll borrow from the Bank of England! I only do freelance work for the *Guardian*, alas, but they may take a couple of articles. Enough to make a short trip out there worthwhile. I'm happy to stay at the backpackers if you have one nearby. Let me know.

I'm forwarding further information on our group and a response to the rest of your questions with it. Please feel free to ask me any more questions.

I'm also interested in your storytelling group, Siliyik. The one you mentioned in the article for the *Feminist News*. I got interested in storytelling at Greenham. We'd sit around the fires at night or in tents in the freezing cold, huddled up in our sleeping bags, and tell stories. I learned more in that

14

time about people than I did in my whole life before that or at university. I'm sure you know what I mean. I believe that storytelling has a transformative power, is a process that allows people to receive and remember the information. What do you think about this?

Thanks again for your long letter and for taking my request seriously. I know I have a lot to learn—but I am willing to put myself on the line to do it. One way or another, we'll drag this old Tory Ship into the late twentieth century. Sometimes I feel I'm on an old creaky sailing ship that still lists in the water in a storm, still relies on servants to set the sails even as they are jumping ship daily. I'm not sure we always know where we're heading. Do you ever feel like that? I know I am being very personal here. Far be it for an English person to get personal! But I learned at Greenham how to let down the barriers, ask questions, begin to move forward. It's essential to break down the old guard. I hope you don't mind. I feel I know you a little from your articles published here. Do let me know if I have spoken out of turn.

I must away. Got to do us bits 'n' bobs in town. I look forward to your reply. I can come in late January if you are able to find some free time then.

Warm regards,

Sahara Green.

He pokeke Uenuku i tu ai.
Against a dark cloud the rainbow stands out
brightly.

"Hey, Iri, get a load of this! A Pommy journo wants to come out here to suss out our nuke-free movement."

Irihapeti is planting new seedlings. "Forget it Cowrie. It'll be the usual *Well gee, how fascinating that you want to keep your quaint Pacific ways but isn't it time you joined the real world of the late twentieth century.*"

"I'm not sure, Iri. This woman has at least done her time at Greenham Common, which means she's had the guts to give up her income to fight for the issues."

"Yeah—probably one of those upper-class Pommy sheilas who has done a turn at varsity and a few months at Greenham and now she's wondering how to get her paper to pay for a visit to the South Pacific." She bends down to scoop up the compost that has slid out the corner of the bag.

"C'mon, Iri. Shouldn't we give her a chance? How will we get our voices into the northern hemisphere unless we learn to work with the women up there? At least she's interested in the issues and we don't have to start from scratch."

"Yeah—or she could be a card-bearing dyke from Leeds with her own political agenda. Can just see how well Te Kotuku would take to that!" Iri laughs, teasing Cowrie.

"Not likely if she works for the *Guardian*! Besides, I doubt that she'd want to hang out here. I think she just

16

wants to be pointed in the right direction. I'll write and suss her out."

"Like, how many goddess tattoos she's got emblazoned on her body and what kind of a labrys she wears around her neck?"

"Iri, you're incorrigible. The last thing I want is a lover. Peta still hangs about my soul and my work at Te Kotuku takes up all my time now. That's enough for me."

"Sorry. Cowrie. I was just teasing you! I know you're passionate about wanting to get our issues north, though I dunno why sometimes. Half the pakeha in Aotearoa don't give a stuff."

"Gotta work on all fronts, Iri. This is an opportunity to advance our work in the Empire—and the coloniser in me, my British whakapapa, cries out for such revenge. This will be sweet work, believe me!" Cowrie leans over to smell the fragrant gardenia revealing its stark white flowers nakedly beside her.

"Trust you to take it up as a challenge, Cowrie! You'd better suss this Brit out before you pour heaps of energy into the cause. Let me know her reply!" Irihapeti places the last of the seedlings in the row and brushes the remaining dirt down her dungarees.

Cowrie strolls back to her nikau hut. She drafts a letter to the journalist, Sahara Green. Interesting name. Maybe she's got African or West Indian blood? She chuckles to herself. Can't wait to see Iri's face if a West Indian Brit turns up. That'll show her! Cowrie drafts a raft of questions that will test the authenticity of the journo—or put her off. Either way, she needs to be sure if she's going to pass on contacts. She chucks the letter onto her desk—a slice of macrocarpa trunk held up by manuka stumps—and strolls over to the Tainui to see if Kuini's into gathering mussels for tea.

17

Haere i mua i te aroaro o Atutahi.
When you travel, go ahead of Atutahi.*

"Hey, Iri, reckon this Sahara Green might be ok!"

Irihapeti pokes her nose up from the nursery account book and looks blankly at Cowrie. "Who the hell is Sahara Green?"

"That Pom who wrote about wanting to bring our nuke-free Pacific into the Empire!"

"Oh, yeah. Her. What's the story?"

Cowrie reads the email. Gradually Iri takes more interest as she listens. "Sappho at Island, eh Cowrie? That proves she's a dyke. Honestly!"

Cowrie grins. "Yeah—but that's not the point."

"Ok. Read on." Cowrie reaches the end of the email. Irihapeti plays with the edges of her account book, grinning.

"What's that smile for, Iri?"

"Think about it, Turtle. She's not just interested in getting these Pacific stories and reading your work. She's sussing you out too."

"Whad'ya mean?"

"Sometimes you are so naive. She's checking out to see if you are a dyke and letting you know she is, silly!"

*Atutahi is the star Canopus. So: go before Canopus appears, while food is still plentiful.

18

"Oh, yeah. Maybe so. But I reckon she's genuine in her aims."

"Oh, Cowrie. Gimme a break. She's out for a South Sea holiday at your expense and reckons if she can fling in an affair it'd be worthwhile too, ya silly old moo!"

Cowrie looks puzzled. "No, I don't think so. I know Brits well enough to know they don't open out that easily. I think she's genuine. Besides, she won't get near me. I'm totally into my work at present. Enjoying my hard-won celibacy and ain't no Pommy broad gonna do me out of it!"

Irihapeti grins. "I always know I can get a rise out of you, Cowrie. To be honest, this sheila sounds half-pie ok. For a Pom, that is! And a journo. I'd rather put my trust in a used-car salesman."

"Like that creepy oil-smeared Philippe at Hokianga Motors? The one who uses his French accent to chat up the ladies?"

"You got it! Last week I saw him slide his hand over Mrs Hohepa's bottom. She flew into a rage and lashed out at him, knocking over the oil can. He had to clean oil from the side of her car while she watched and the other patrons laughed. Serve the bugger right!"

"Every time I see those ads for holidays in the South of France I visualise a hundred greasy little Philippes with octopus hands all over the place. The holiday from hell!"

"You racist old tart. Not all Frogs are like that."

"Too right. Some of them creep up on us in inflatables in the dark of the night and attach bombs to the side of our boats."

"Yeah, then get a holiday on Hau Atoll for their sins and after the break, a hero's welcome back home in France from that creepy little Chirac who engineered their escape."

"It's hard to trust any of the bastards after that drama, eh? I try not to be prejudiced, but I still can't buy French wine all these years later."

"I don't reckon they'll ever know how strongly we feel about them in the Pacific. They're worse than the Brits in terms of holding onto the last vestiges of colonial power. They've got the Tahitians totally dependent on them, working for them and speaking their own language. It'll be years before independence hits their shores. Hey, help me cart these bags of compost while you're here, Cowrie. I didn't expect the boys to pack up 40-pound bags. I can manage the others on my own but these'll kill my back."

"Sure, Iri. So long as you stop teasing me about the Pom!"

"Sappho at Island, indeed! I'm quite looking forward to meeting her, actually."

"Ah, so it was a bit of projection then, eh, Iri? A while since you've had a lover." Now it's Cowrie's turn to tease her mate and she launches in relentlessly, enjoying the boot being on the other foot. After half an hour, all the bags of compost have been moved from the storehouse into the nursery and they break for a cuppa.

From: koana@hilo.com
To: turtle@hokianga.co.nz

Aloha Turtle,

Mahalo for your email. Great to catch up on the news. Have much to tell you. At Kanaka Maoli meeting last night Mauva from Tahiti Fa'a'a spoke. Some of the men working at the Moruroa test site reckon the French are gearing up for more tests at Moruroa. They should know! Evidently, the official line is to neither confirm nor deny but they've dug new shafts and some say it could be a dozen or so underground tests. We've sent a letter to Chirac demanding to know the truth of the reports but it's unlikely he'll even respond. Have you heard anything down in Aotearoa? Keep it quiet as yet. We're still deciding what action to take if they go ahead. Some say they simply wouldn't be allowed to. World opinion has changed so much since their last tests. But then again, you know the French government! Who'd have thought they'd actually assign agents to blow up the *Rainbow Warrior*? It's outrageous. Email if you know anything.

I've finally given up my job at the post office. I'm working full time for Kanaka Maoli and we're steaming ahead. I'm also helping Pele Aloha document the stories of three generations of Hawai'ians. We're sailing over to Kauai next week to work for two weeks. So try to call me before I leave if you know anything. Otherwise, I'll assume you don't.

Peni, Nele and Ela send aloha—also Paneke and Keo. They came down for dinner last night and we recalled that evening I taught you hula. Did we laugh! Mind you, I'm not so hot on waiata—so I guess I can't talk! Paneke took Mauva and a small group of Tahitians through the Kiluaea crater.

One of them nearly slipped into the steam vent near Halema'uma'u. Close call. Pele never lets us forget her presence!

Thank Kuini for the email about Te Aroha. I've passed the information to Ela and the group at Hilo. They reckon the programme could be adapted successfully here. Many similar issues. Ela is becoming more involved with her women's group for survivors. Her friends in Texas say Chad's got back into the booze in a big way and is totally into denial. Ela, however, has used the experience as a springboard into a new future. Her confidence grows daily. But she is still fragile inside. Some days she's like a nautilus shell, papery thin and easily crushed. The kids are pretty good about it though. They see the signs and tend to steer clear or go quiet. We usually give her space when she needs it.

We live together well. Nothing romantic—which I may have wanted once—but she is a superb person to share a house with and all our kids get on. Meantime, I'm getting quite close to Kehaulani. Remember, she was the woman who first took me swimming where Pele's lava gushes into the ocean? The same place I took you on your last visit. We're working together on documenting historical land rights. Her job as a guide at Volcano National Park has helped because she has access to all sorts of government documents we might find it hard to get our hands on!

We've both joined the Punalu'u canoe club. We keep our canoes in the lagoon and race off shore. All sorts from original waka to modern versions and even some outriggers from Samoa and the Cooks. It's kamaha'o. Hey—you know those seeds and plants Irihapeti sent through for Paneke? Well, the US customs thought they were dak and confiscated them. What a joke! Imagine someone sending marijuana from Aotearoa to Hawai'i? This is the home of the best dak in the world. Many of our people are now reliant on it to earn a living, thanks to the US colonisers. And they imagine we'd all be silly enough to send it in a bag marked "Rare plants—Do Not Open!" We had a good laugh though! Eventually, Keo had to go to the Federal Drug and Alcohol Unit to collect what was left of the seeds. The plants had karked it! So tell Iri to send more— but make sure she gets customs clearance at that end so they don't hassle us! Mahalo!

Hope life at Te Kotuku is kamaha'o. Sounds like you're working hard but managing to fit in some fun. Do tell us more about that English haole! We could send her information but Pele Aloha wants you to suss her out for us first. We don't want our words mangled into British English and splashed all over the *Guardian*. Or the *Sun*! I bet they don't realise we know about all their sleazy little tabloids. *Hard Copy* is the most watched programme on the island! We reckon they sent out the missionaries as the first point of indoctrination and the television sets as the next!

Hey—when are you coming back to see us? We'll have fresh ahi cooked in banana leaves and poi ready! I know the way to tempt you is through your sensuous tastes, Cowrie! I can't wait to savour that smoked kahawai you keep raving to us about. The fishing trip you did recently with Kuini sounded fantastic. We love being out in the canoes at sunset. Last week, we had turtles swimming alongside us as we came back into the Punalu'u lagoon. I thought of you!

Aloha to all at Te Kotuku,

Koana.

23

He peka titoki e kore e whati.
A branch of the titoki tree will not break.

At the next iwi gathering, Piripi confirms reports from Tahitian Maoris working at Moruroa Atoll that the French will be resuming underground nuclear tests. The iwi are horrified and korero focuses on the effects this will have for the entire Pacific. Plans are made to set up a group to monitor the situation. Cowrie, Kuini, Mere, Irihapeti, Piripi, Hemi and Eruera are elected.

The following day, Cowrie emails Koana to confirm the reports and ask her to stay in touch on Kanaka Maoli action. The Indigenous Peoples' Network is already buzzing with information and yet there has not yet been an official announcement from the French, who are still maintaining their neither-confirm-nor-deny tactics.

Kuini returns from a Te Aroha case at Kaitaia and after work they roast kumara over the fire with a group of women from the writers' hui. Their meetings are only twice monthly but none of them would miss the sharing of stories for anything. They discuss possible action if the French resume tests and agree that a contingent of local iwi should sponsor a boat, possibly a waka, to protest at Moruroa, to enter the exclusion zone if necessary.

"I'd like to see women on board even though it has traditionally been men," suggests Irihapeti. "Women have long been the peacemakers, in the war against pakeha landgrabbers and invaders, in two world wars. We have a trusted tradition of peaceful protest."

"Yeah, if Greenpeace has a mixed crew, isn't it time we came on board also?" Kuini points out.

All but two of the women agree. They decide to put it to the larger iwi protest group.

After the hui, Kuini, Irihapeti and Cowrie meet in the Tainui housetruck for manuka tea.

"My dream is to see a waka entirely paddled by wahine from all the Pacific Islands enter the test zone. Imagine the response. The world's media would be hovering above in awe."

"Yeah—and we'd have half of those missionary-sodden Tahitians, the ones indoctrinated with French Christian values, telling us we have betrayed indigenous Pacific roots. That's not such a good idea," adds Kuini.

"But just imagine the power of the image! That'd speak more than words."

"It'd sure have impact!"

"Yeah, but remember that the twelve-mile exclusion zone is quite a way from the atoll. It'd be helluva rough out there and risky unless we had a support boat."

"Like the *Rainbow Warrior*?"

"Maybe we should link in with the Greenpeace women as a women's solidarity issue?"

"But that'd alienate many of the local iwi. I think we need to hear what actions are planned, then discuss where we go from there."

"And we're not totally sure that the tests will take place. I mean, it's only rumour right now. None of the French have confirmed it."

"Yeah, but since when was bush telegraph wrong on these issues? I trust the fellas at Moruroa. Most of the Maohi working there hate the nuclear test site but know it's the only way they can feed their families while the French remain. Maybe this'll be the turning point?"

Cowrie lights up the gas cooker for a second round of the sweet fragrant tea. She takes several sprigs of manuka flowers and leaves, and places them in the bottom of the clay pot, ready for the boiling water to seep through.

"Well, I don't think we should abandon the idea yet. Let's keep it brewing huh?" Iri suggests.

They sip their manuka tea, letting it seep into their blood. The moon hangs high above the dunes and a lone ruru call spikes the night air with its echo.

E ai o harirau?
What wings do you have with which to fly here?

"Tell us how Maui got the bone fishhook, Cowrie."

The kohanga kids have heard this many times before, but never tire of the story. Cowrie settles them down after a day of learning to fish using traditional bone and paua hooks. They are entranced and ready to rest since they've been cavorting up and down the dunes all morning, throwing their baited lines into the sea, pretending to catch a huge octopus and various other taniwha and sea monsters.

Cowrie explains how Maui-tikitiki-a-Taranga had been with his parents in the underworld and how he learned to cheat his ancestor Muriranga-whenua of food in order to get her jawbone, which he knew was enchanted. Once he had it, he carved it into a fishhook and went out in his canoe and fished up the Great Fish of Aotearoa—the North Island. "See the ika? Here's the tail and here's the head," says Cowrie, showing them a map of the island in the shape of a fish.

"Didn't he also make a mere from the bone to slow down the sun?" asks Maata.

"Ae." Cowrie finishes the tale and asks them each to tell a story about Maui, whom they all know and love because he is the trickster, the wise fool, the coyote of their ancestry. They like it when he assumes different shapes and especially when he does so to spy on his parents. That is always calculated to get their attention.

28

The afternoon rolls on, the kohanga kids eventually retiring to draw their own impressions of Maui fishing up the land from the ocean and pulling back the sun to slow it down.

After kohanga, she strolls to the Tainui to see if Kuini is back from the Te Aroha session at Rawene. Kuini arrives just as she enters the housetruck.

"Cowrie. It's all on. The bastards have done it. I can't believe it. Bloody rapists!"

Cowrie is stunned, wondering if it's a local case of gang rape. Unusual for Kuini to loose her cool. She deals with this stuff every day.

"They never bloody learn. You'd think multiple rape would teach them, but it's had no effect at all." Kuini is distraught and angry at once.

Cowrie guides her to the housetruck and lights the gas for a cuppa while Kuini gets her breath back. "Who's upset you so much? A local fella?"

"Shouldn't bloody be anywhere near our shores, let alone with his dick inside them."

Cowrie holds back, knowing Kuini will calm down and tell her soon. She's not sure she wants to hear which monster has done this to a local wahine. She pours hot water over the sliced ginger and adds a teaspoon of pohutukawa honey to the brew. By this time Kuini has calmed down a little.

"Kuini. Who is it? Do I know him?"

"Not personally, but you bloody well know his kind."

"Well who? Local iwi?"

"Na, bloody foreign iwi. It's that fuckin' Chirac. First he insults us by letting the *Rainbow Warrior* French agents free after they bombed us—and now he's at it again. It's all true. Heard it on the truck radio on my way back. The French have announced they are resuming

29

nuclear bomb tests on Moruroa Atoll between September this year and March next year. I never really believed they'd have the bloody gall to do it."

"De Gaulle! He started it all!" Cowrie can't help herself. "Jeez, so the bush telegraph was right. I knew it. I must talk to Koana and see what they know. Mauva and the Tahitian storytellers are still in Hawai'i with her."

"They'll know by now, Cowrie. It was on every news station I tuned in to. They even interrupted a bloody rugby match to announce it—and you know how sacred that is. We can't let it go ahead. We have to do everything to stop the tests. Bugger the protocol. I'm ready to sail a waka right into the test zone now ..."

Cowrie sits in stunned silence. She's been preparing herself for this—but she never thought that even the French would have the arrogance and disrespect to resume nuclear testing in the Pacific. They'd agreed to sign the Nuclear Non-Proliferation Treaty along with most of the rest of the world, finally—and everyone thought that'd be the end of it. Except the Tahitians, of course. They always said it was just a break, that they didn't trust their colonisers. Now it's true.

Kuini is still muttering and swearing as she makes notes about whom to call and what action to take. Irihapeti joins them, having just heard the news up at the wharenui. "Hey, Cowrie, you'd better get that Pommy sheila down here for some action. The English were masters in the art of colonisation. Taught it to the rest of the world. Reckon it should be right up her alley, her responsibility, as her letter implied, to come and report it back to her people."

"Too bloody right," agrees Kuini. "Reckon she'd be on board, Cowrie?"

"I dunno. She was going to come in the summer."

"Yeah, for a bloody holiday and to escape the British winter, eh?" says Iri.

Cowrie shoots her a glare from the corner of her eyes. "This is a test for us. I reckon we need all the support we can get from international media for this battle. We need to work together as women too. Remember how we distrusted the women at Greenham initially but many of them lasted longer out in the cold than we expected."

"Spoken like a real trooper, Cowrie. You should be a bloody politician!" Kuini laughs.

Iri and Kuini agree that it's worth giving Sahara a chance if she's willing to come. Maybe Greenpeace UK will chip in for her fare? They discuss other courses of action, then split to organise a meeting at the wharenui after dinner. Everyone will attend. There's not a single family living on the marae and surrounding villages who'd miss the action. Everyone feels strongly about the rape of te whenua—the earth, about the fact that it would not be happening if it weren't for a foreign government which has outlived its stay in the Pacific.

Tunu huruhuru, kei wawe tu ana a Pu-whakaoho.
Cook it with its hair on, lest you be interrupted by
Pu-whakaoho.

She strolls over the dunes in the haunting moonlight,
toward a cave at the mouth of the harbour. From within,
voices, waiata. Then silence. She enters the cave, drawn
by a power from within. At the far end, a pinpoint of
light. She walks toward it. Nearing, she sees a rounded
piece of bone, light shining from its centre. It appears
suspended in mid-air. She moves closer. The bone hovers
at eye level. She reaches out her hand. The bone is placed
in her palm. It is in the shape of a fishhook. Light shines
through the ribs of the old kuia. A piece of one rib is
missing.

Cowrie looks down. Her own hei matau lies safe on
her breastbone, next to the carved turtle. She clutches it
in comfort. A warm glow emanates from the bone, heat-
ing her hand. She lies awake, the moon slanting down
through the nikau trunks, lying across her body like bars.
Then she remembers Moruroa. Invasion. Rape. They
tunnel shafts deep into Papatuanuku, put nuclear explosives capable of another Hiroshima into them, blast
apart the atoll, and say that the tests are totally safe. She
moans, turns over, but cannot sleep. She tries to imagine
sailing a waka into the test zone, women from all the
islands on board. Gradually, her body begins to relax and
she falls into a deep sleep.

This time she is fishing. Using the bone hook given to
her in the cave. She feels a tug at the other end of the line.

Imagining a beautiful fresh ika, she reels in her catch. It gets heavier and heavier as she pulls the fish to the surface. The ika struggles wildly, flops out into the waka, its mouth open, gasping for breath, then releases a baby from its gullet. Cowrie bends down to examine it more closely. The fish has no tail, no eyes. It looks like an amoeba. She holds it up to the light and gasps. It is a half-formed human baby with no arms or legs. Just a belly and traces of a human face. She screams, dropping the baby. It sinks to the ocean depths.

Cowrie wakes, disturbed. She cannot go back to sleep. She gets up and throws on her lavalava. An ancient weta watches from the foot of her bed, casting its antennae out to see what her reactions will be. She takes a deep breath and walks past the creature toward the Tainui. Kuini is reading by candlelight. She taps at the window and Kuini lets her in.

Cowrie recounts her nightmare. Kuini sits in silence. "However you interpret it, Cowrie, this is a call to action. We can't ignore it."

"I was telling the kohanga kids about Muriranga-whenua giving her jawbone to Maui today—so I think that was swirling around in my head. And the testaments given by the elders who visited Rongelap after the last tests and saw the jellyfish babies. I don't want to go back to sleep alone. Ok if I stay here?"

"Sure thing, sis. Come and cuddle up." Kuini holds open her tapa-patterned sheet and Cowrie nuzzles in beside her. They discuss stories about the tests until they are so exhausted they drift into a deep sleep.

From: sappho@island.ac.uk
To: turtle@hokianga.co.nz

Dear Cowrie,

I am shocked to hear the announcement from President
Chirac that the French are planning a series of nuclear
explosions in French Polynesia. I feel called to action. We
cannot just stand aside and do nothing here in Britain.
Our own conservation and anti-nuclear groups in the UK
are pressuring Major to respond, but so far he refuses to
commit himself. There are messages of outrage coming from
Germany, Holland, Belgium and the rest of Europe but still
our government remains silent. Hopefully, public pressure will
change that.

I've approached the *Guardian* for funding to cover events in
the South Pacific since there will clearly be a long period of
protest if the tests go ahead. Let's hope we can stop them
before that occurs. They said they'd take freelance articles
if I make it over there. And the women's support network of
anti-nuclear and political lobbies are pooling resources for
campaigns of protest here and say they'd be willing to
donate something toward the trip.

Dad's managed to borrow funds against his home. He
bought it back from the council three years ago. He's all for
me coming. I'm surprised, since some members of his union
still believe in weapons as a deterrent. However, they're
against colonial power. See it as an extension of the regime
of the bosses over workers. They had a rally on the weekend
and the funds raised will go towards their union campaign
against the tests—but they've earmarked 10 per cent for
every article I write opposing the tests. I was so touched

when I heard that, I cried. You have to know them to realise what a commitment this is. Most of the quarry workers live hand to mouth, work long hours and just manage to support their families. It's made me more determined to come, to cover the issues as best I can and try to motivate Britain into action. No small task, I can tell you! Mind you, Dad did say the fact that the French have major shares in the quarry and have made working conditions worse since taking it over has helped motivate their anger!

Dad's quite strongly anti-French. Partly because of that and maybe since Mum took off to Paris after they split up. I tried to argue that us Brits have as bad a record of colonialism but he reckons we did it without the arrogance of the French. The quarry workers held a demonstration when it was revealed that the French government had ordered their own agents to sink the *Rainbow Warrior*. Mind you, as he said, it was as much against their new French bosses as the frogmen downunder!

But I deviate from the reason for this email. I have changed plans so I can come to the South Pacific for a longer period and cover the protest movement from as many angles as possible. I am committed to this. But I will need your help when I arrive in making contacts that can provide an indigenous perspective and maybe in sailing on a protest boat to Moruroa. Greenpeace need independent media since they will surely sail into the exclusion zone and be boarded, even taken captive. It has happened there before.

I realise I am asking a great deal from you. Thank you for your trust in me so far and your long letter explaining the background to the tests in the Pacific. I really appreciate this. And you can tell Irihapeti, no, I am not just coming for a South Pacific holiday! At first I was hurt by the suggestion, but I can see where she's coming from. I can think of far easier ways to holiday than by stretching myself to understand these issues better, by risking the journey to the edge of the test zone! I'm forwarding some previous work to put your own and Irihapeti's mind at rest. They begin with the Greenham protests and cover the miners' strike and a range of other issues. Let me know what you think.

Thanks for everything—Sahara.

p.s. Last night I dreamed I was sailing in warm waters. It was idyllic. Then there was an explosion. Hundreds of dead fish emerged from the depths, floating around us. The smell was horrendous. I woke with a nasty taste in my mouth. I know this has happened before. It must never happen again.

pps. I also dreamed of cooking fish on the beach with you. They were sweet and delicious. That was the night before. We must keep this hope alive too. Your letter really got me thinking. You have set dark barges adrift within me. Thank you for taking me from the safe cocoon of my thoughts into your underwater world.

Warm wishes—and pleasant dreams!—Sahara.

Aroha mai, aroha atu.
Love toward us, love going out from us.

"Warm thoughts and pleasant dreams, eh? Sounds like she's ready to snuggle up with you already, Cowrie. Very cosy," adds Irihapeti, trying to get a rise out of her friend.

"Come on, we don't even know if she's a dyke, and in any case she sounds like she's genuinely interested in the cause and she's done her homework." Kuini knows what Irihapeti is after and short-circuits the response.

"Of course she is. Sappho at Island, indeed," replies Irihapeti smiling.

"I don't care how gorgeous she is. I'm focused on stopping these tests. Besides, I'm not really over Peta yet. She still smoulders away in my soul. Iri, you're incorrigible."

"Yeah, but I know you like the sound of this Sahara. I saw the light in your eyes when you read the bit about her dream."

"Yeah, real romantic sailing amongst stinking fish that have been nuked by the French," adds Kuini.

"Na, I was referring to the second one—cooking up fish on the beach with Cowrie. She's probably really cute, spiky mop, and dying to get into a kayak, let alone share succulent kina with our Cowrie! I can just see them now roasting kina and kumara on the dunes, the orange glow of the sun setting on the far horizon, a strange light in the distance. They imagine a dark barge turning into a

37

shooting star, then suddenly, there it is, Moruroa erupting out of the water, flashing up into a vibrant sky!"

"Iri, that's tasteless even for you," admonishes Kuini. But they laugh.

"Ok, lay off! This visit is strictly business. Yes—I do admit this woman interests me. She's intelligent, vibrant, political, has the guts to question the colonial system when she could just sit back and rake in its benefits, and I'm interested in anyone who could write 'you have set dark barges adrift in me.' There's more to her than meets the eye. But I have no desire to get involved beyond our work. I'm overcommitted as it is."

"Famous last words! Bet you'd love to be one of those dark barges floating around in her sensuous seas. I see a moonlit trip down the English canals toward Stratford-upon-Avon, Cowrie at the helm. I hear Vivaldi in the background—no, Elgar. Has to be a Pom. Sailing toward the roots of civilisation, Shakespeare, nay, maybe even the bed of Ann Hathaway. More likely on reflection ..." A spray of sand covers Iri's face before she can finish and gets between her teeth, causing her to throw more sand back at Cowrie.

Kuini intervenes before her seedbed is splattered across the Tainui. "Whakamutu! That sand holds my new seeds. Settle down, sisters!"

Irihapeti agrees not to bait Cowrie. "Sorry, mate. It's just that you usually get interested in women when you're overseas on your studies and this is the first time I've seen your eyes light up like that."

"Yeah—but what you should remember is her beadies light up at the prospect of political action too, Iri. Come on, you fellas, let's get back to the topic of how we can best make use of the Pom while she's here. She'll be vital to get our voices into the UK and she is familiar with the issues already. That's one hell of a start when you're dealing with those northern hemisphere broads." They laugh at her reclamation of familiar terms.

The rest of the afternoon is spent pooling resources and networks to make sure the journalist speaks to a range of people over her time in Aotearoa and seeing how she can fit into their own protest plans. They discuss the wider issues and delegate work for contacting media and checking to see if the local women's branch of Greenpeace will be sending a delegate on board the Peace Flotilla to protest at Moruroa. Afterwards, they fry wheke over the fire, drooling as the tentacles crisp up in the heat, drawing in the orange and mango juices, preparing themselves for the sampling.

He harore rangi tahi.
A mushroom of a single day.

Two weeks later Cowrie is standing at Arrivals in the Jean Batten wing of the international air terminal, named after a famous local aviatrix who Iri also thought was a dyke. The British Airways flight disgorges pale bodies of people who appear too tired to care. In their eyes, a world-weariness born of inner city grind. So much for the romance of the airline ads. Nice steward though. Very camp. His boyfriend greets him, whisks him away before she can get closer look. A sweet couple emerge, holding photos of their grandchildren. They are immediately enveloped in kisses from the waiting families. Now there's a spunky woman. Wonder if that's her? She looks into her eyes as the woman spies her lover in the distance, and runs to greet her. More people spill through customs. Cowrie's brow creases. God, hope she didn't bring in any dak. I should have warned her about how strict New Zealand customs are. Then again, she wouldn't be that naive being a journo, surely? Her eyes trail over the last straggling arrivals when an energetic spiky-haired dyke blasts through the doors, looking about for her host. Sharp green eyes. She feels a jolt within. "Sahara?" she asks.

"Yes. Hi! You must be Cowrie," she ventures, a pleasant lisp in her speech. Very cute. Cowrie braces herself. She knows, beyond all doubt, she could never fall for a Pom, no matter how bright she is.

"Kia ora. Welcome to Aotearoa." Cowrie hangs a lei around her neck, a garland of dried pohutukawa interwoven with nikau palm leaves.

Sahara looks pleased. "Wow! Did you make this?"

Cowrie blushes. "No big deal. Hey—let's get out of here. I hate airports."

"Yes, I'm bushed. I had a long train ride to Heathrow then a three-hour delay. When I finally got on board, I was next to an overbearing businessman who tried to sell me little painted statues of the Virgin Mary. He imports them from China and sells them to the South Africans. Does a roaring trade evidently. Thought I'd be perfect to join him out there."

"Oh, Pele preserve me. What did you say to him?"

"Another time, maybe."

Cowrie is surprised. No dyke in Aotearoa would be that polite. Trust the Poms. I guess it's in their genes. "Very noble of you. I'd have dropped my hot dinner in his crotch and warned him that was just the first course."

"Really? I must admit, I didn't think of doing that." Sahara laughs nervously, wondering if she'd really do this or she'd just fantasise doing it.

By now they have walked over to the rows of vehicles. Cowrie points to the van at the end with "Te Aroha, Te Kotuku, Hokianga" written on it. "That's our wagon, Sahara, so hitch up your camels and we'll be off. How did you get that name, by the way?"

"It's a long story. I'll tell you once we're on the way. Is it far to the Hokianga?"

Cowrie visualises the long, winding road through the Waipoua Forest and chuckles. "Not far in a straight line, but since I always take the bent route, it could be a few hours. Mind you—it's a stunning journey. And we'll need to visit Tane Mahuta to pay our respects before you enter the harbour."

"Really? Couldn't we visit her tomorrow? I must admit, I'm really beat."

Cowrie laughs. "Tane Mahuta is a he—God of the kauri forest, actually—and he's right on our route. You'll be ready for a welcome break by then and we shouldn't pass without paying our respects."

"Oh, I see. That's fine then. Sorry."

"It's ok. How were you to know?"

"What time is it here? I should adjust my watch."

"Only nine-thirty in the morning. We've missed the rush-hour traffic, such as it is in Auckland. The locals complain but it's nothing next to two hours on the San Francisco Bay Bridge getting home from work. Now, you gonna tell me how you got that name?"

Sahara settles into her seat and explains how her mother had returned from visiting her father who at that time worked as foreman for the quarry in a township near the Sahara Desert. She named the child Sahara, hoping the birth would bring the romance back into the relationship with Sahara's father. It did, for a time. Then her mother got fed up and left. "So I was named after the mighty dunes she loved so much. My strongest memory is her talking to me about those dunes. They were like huge mountains of hope for her." Sahara is silent for a while. Cowrie drives on, amazed at the spirited language of this woman, her recourse to poetry in her speech, even jet-lagged. Like the dark barges of her letter. Beyond the usual journalistic jargon.

Sahara nods off as they pass through the kumara country of Ruawai and the ochre waters of the river running beside them. Before long, they are parked at the pathway to pay homage to Tane Mahuta. Sahara wakes, missing the purring of the motor. "Wow! This looks like virgin rainforest. Last time I was awake we were passing rolling hills that reminded me of England. Parwich, near my dad's home. But this is incredible."

"Wanna see the real thing?"

"You bet. Time for a wee walk. Is it far?"

"No—but you might wanna bring your camera."

"It's buried deep in my pack. Besides, I'd rather remember it in spirit," she replies. Cowrie likes her attitude. She's warming to this Brit by the minute.

They walk along a narrow dirt path, surrounded by native trees which she names for Sahara. They round a bend and suddenly, towering above them, is the gigantic girth of the God of the kauri forest. Sahara gasps. "I have never seen anything like this. His branches are so high up you can hardly see them. He must be as wide as ten cars. More?"

Cowrie nods, as they move toward the huge trunk. Sahara's eyes widen to take in the massive sight. She bends forward, then suddenly falls onto the wooden platform which protects the tree roots. Cowrie takes her head in her lap, pours water from her hip flask down her cheeks. Sahara does not move. Too jet-lagged. But she is still breathing. After a while, she murmurs, surfacing from the heat, the shock. She looks up. Cowrie notices her jade green eyes are open, vulnerable, beautiful.

Te taepaepatanga o te rangi.
The place where the sky hangs down to the horizon.

"So Tane Mahuta really wowed you, eh Sahara?" Kuini chuckles as she passes kai from the hangi to a rather dazzled Sahara, talk of the marae since her dramatic arrival was broadcast through the community.

"I'd like to think it was jet-lag and heat but I must admit, that Tree God is spectacular to say the least." Sahara smiles. The last thing she remembered was a silver starfish in the corner of Cowrie's eye as she drifted out of the forest and into another world. She felt she was swimming, drowning, then she was lifted up, as if onto the back of a dolphin or turtle, and brought in safely to land. She woke up thinking she was in heaven, the sun streaming through the nikau walls of the hut. Cowrie was there at her bedside, pouring mango juice onto her parched tongue from a half coconut shell. Once she drained the liquid, a woman in the shape of a turtle emerged from the interior husk of the shell. Then she fell back into a deep sleep.

"I have to admit, I teased Cowrie about you coming, but I didn't expect quite such a dramatic entrance, especially for a Brit!" admits Irihapeti. Cowrie glares at her.

Sahara notices. "It's ok. I'm used to it. I feel the same about England. But we'll oust the Tories at the next election. I'm determined to look forward with hope."

"She's got it sussed," whispers Kuini. "Just the

woman for us!" She swigs the last of the feijoa wine and burps gloriously.

Sahara can more than hold her own with the wild women of Te Kotuku. At first, Cowrie feels protective towards her, but soon realises she is quite capable of looking after herself. Her time at Greenham Common would have prepared her. That community had its own kind of tribal bonding.

After kai, Kuini, Iri, Cowrie and Sahara walk over the dunes to the beach, light a fire and discuss plans for the protest movement. Mattiu has offered his fishing trawler as one of the craft to be witness at the twelve-mile exclusion zone outside Moruroa Atoll and Piripi says some Cook Island rellies are planning to sail a canoe from their shores in protest. He's keen on paddling a waka over, but knows the journey could be hazardous with the mid-season weather patterns. Meanwhile, Oscar Temaru and others from Tavini Haraatira, the Tahitian Independence Movement, have requested support for marches they plan over the course of the tests, for as long as it takes to retain world-wide media attention on their cause.

"So, where do you see your skills helping most, Sahara?" asks Kuini.

"I'll be guided by you all in this, but I'd like to report back the issues to Europe and Britain. They only see it as a protest over nuclear testing. The question of French colonisation of Tahiti is not widely known."

"So, we need to get Sahara over to Tahiti, as well as covering the story from here. That means on one of the boats or by flying into Fa'a'a and joining the resistance movement from the land," Cowrie offers.

Over the next three hours, they map out a number of possible plans to bring to the meeting in two days time.

The fire burns down to bright embers which just keep them warm enough. Irihapeti and Kuini return to the marae, leaving Cowrie and Sahara to walk the beach by the light of the sickle moon. Cowrie splashes her feet in the water, revealing magic shards of silver that spring up from the mercury reflected in the moonlight. Sahara is entranced. Floating in a shallow rock pool is a feather starfish, its fairy tentacles lit up by the spray of light reflected in the pond. "She's dancing in the moonwater. Look at her, so live and free. I long to be like that." A tear emerges from the corner of Sahara's eye. Cowrie is moved by the open tenderness of this new creature who has entered her life, so unexpectedly, so sensitively. She squeezes her hand softly.

They return to the nikau hut refreshed, elated, ready for the challenges ahead. Cowrie drifts off to sleep on the mat next to Sahara, wondering if she has a girlfriend in Britain who is missing her now, but not wanting to ask, to destroy her warm dreams. Not tonight, anyway.

From: notests@tahiti.com
To: turtle@hokianga.co.nz

Aloha Cowrie—

I have just returned from visiting Koana and working with
Kanaka Maoli movement to find that, despite all their
promises, the government is about to blast apart our atoll
again. It is bad enough having their presence and language
possessing our lands, but they can take their bloody bombs
back home. I'm so furious. They rape our land. You know they
dig shafts into her, penetrate her body, then shaft her
apart, exploding her, all the time telling us, as if we are
stupid children who cannot understand, that it does no
harm. Worst of all, I still speak their fucking language. Grew
up with it at school. It's like they invade me from the inside.
Tu comprends?

Koana urged me to email you. We need to get indigenous
Pacific women here for the marches we plan in protest.
We hope to stop the the tests proceeding. Can you help us?
Please forward the email following to every group you can.
We welcome all people who can support our cause, but
especially Pacific women.

Koana also said that you'd made contact with a British
journalist who could get our voices into Europe. Can you
send us her email? We need to cast our net as wide as we
can to draw in all the support needed to stop this insanity.
We fear for the future we are raising our children into. I saw
babies from Rongelap with deformed limbs, eyeless sockets,
some hardly recognisable as human. Once you see that, you
never forget it.

They say the tests are safe but all we need is one mistake. We know they've cracked the atoll before and we have photos to prove it. Please help us. Spread our message as far as you can.

Koana sends aloha and tells us you are a wonderful swimmer. Like a turtle, she said. Slow on land but swift in the water. We could use you over here right now! Please email and let me know you got this. Aloha from us all,

Mauva Temaru.

From: turtle@hokianga.co.nz
To: notests@tahiti.com

Kia ora Mauva,

Mahalo for your email. Ae, we're furious too! I'm attaching
a file here to inform you of our planned action. Same
decoding as before. Here at Te Kotuku we want to send a
local fishing trawler with a waka aboard to protest. How
long do you think we have? Is the date of the first test
known yet?

I'm also forwarding information from Sahara Green—the
British journo. She's currently with us on the marae.
You can email her as above.

I saw pictures of deformed infants—'jellyfish babies'—from
the US nuclear tests in the Marshall Islands. I can never
erase them from my heart. We cannot let this happen in
Tahiti. I know there are deformities and cancers already but
the French are still denying the illnesses have anything to
do with the tests. Unreal!

Please let us know what else we can do. I'll keep you
emailed on our movements. Sahara is cool. She can be
trusted to let you speak in your own voices. She
understands about colonisation and wants to help inform
readers in the UK and Europe. She's keen to be aboard one
of the boats, or will report from the land marches. Can you
help ensure this in case our trawler never makes it?
Mahalo.

Please pass on our aroha to your people. We'll get as
many tangata whenua there in support as possible. There

will be widespread protest in Aotearoa. Some are talking about a Peace Flotilla already. Stay in touch. We'll need to act fast.

Ka pai—kia kaha—arohanui from us all—

Cowrie.

Kei muri i te awe kapara he tangata ke, mana te ao, he mu.
Shadowed behind the tattooed face a stranger stands, he who owns the earth, and he is white.

Over the next two weeks, frantic emailing takes place between Tahiti Fa'a'a, Greenpeace Aotearoa, the Tahitian Independence Movement and the range of conservation and peace groups scattered about Aotearoa and the Pacific.

There is only one fishing trawler large enough to take a waka on board to get to the test zone. From there, the waka will encircle the twelve-mile exclusion zone daily, tie up to the trawler for safety and report back to media by night. It will ensure an indigenous presence and attract media attention. There will be representatives from other iwi on board the trawler, some media, and crew. Muriwhenua are in support of the action. Meantime, all over Aotearoa, boaties and sailing clubs, peace movement activists, fishermen and people from all races and classes are pulling together contingents for a Peace Flotilla and continued presence at Moruroa. The aim is to prevent tests from taking place and to keep a vigilant presence should testing happen. Greenpeace stresses that it is vital to keep the world's media attention on the test zone or the battle will be lost.

The first boats in the contingent aim to leave within the next two weeks. The tests are reported to begin in six weeks. They'll stop off at Rarotonga on the way to replenish supplies, join a land march in Tahiti Fa'a'a, then sail for the test zone at Moruroa once enough boats have arrived to create media interest.

Before they leave, Sahara is keen to explore the mighty sand dunes that stretch out beyond Te Kotuku marae. They plan a trek into the seaside desert. "There's a few wrecked English sailing ships up the coastline, so you might meet up with some of your ancestors," Kuini suggests.

Sahara grins. She's getting used to being teased. "Might make good kai for dinner then, aye, Kuini? Like Captain Cook?"

"Never tasted him myself, but I hear from the Hawai'ians he was rather gristly and they had to spit him out," replies Kuini, quick as a flash.

"Na, Tahitians wasn't it?" adds Cowrie.

Kuini turns on her in mock surprise. "C'mon Cowrie. It was your rellies on the Big Island that got to taste him finally. You should be proud of it." Kuini rolls her eyes for good measure and pokes out her tongue as if ending a haka. Sahara is suitably impressed.

"Shit! I really put my foot in it then. I remember telling Nele and Peni he got eaten on a beach in Tahiti. Fancy them believing me. You'd reckon that detail wouldn't be missed in their school books, since the historians love painting us all as cannibals."

"Ya can't cover up your mistake that easily Cowrie. Wait'll I tell Mere. She'll disown ya then," Kuini laughs.

"No way! I've been abandoned by one mother and Mere sure ain't gonna get the chance to do that trip on me, sister." Cowrie covers her vulnerability with bravado.

"C'mon you two. Quit quibbling. Let's get packed for the journey and be off before it gets too hot." Irihapeti grabs a flax kete and starts piling in towels and fishing line.

"What's the string for?" asks Sahara. "Will we go fishing further up the coast?"

"You just wait and see, Sahara," grins Iri. "But I reckon you'll like it."

Sahara is so used to them speaking over top of each other or being enigmatic, a local custom apparently, that she decides not to enquire further. She returns to the nikau hut with Cowrie to grab her backpack. Cowrie watches her piling in gear, then hands over a kete. "You'll find this more comfortable, Sahara. It's made from flax—natural fibre—and doesn't sweat like that plastic stuff. I've made special handles so that it can be used as a pack to free up the arms. " Cowrie indicates the woven straps.

"Wow! This is so beautiful Cowrie. The texture reminds me of dillybags I saw in an Aboriginal weaving exhibition in London."

"Yeah—these are also used for fishing and shellfish as well as hunting and gathering. Make jolly fine head pieces too, old bean, to protect us from the glaring London UV rays." Cowrie mocks a British accent used on television ads and places a kete over her head, strutting out the hut door as if she is modelling a new hat for Christian Dior.

Sahara grins. "You've got the Pommy accent down well, Cowrie."

"BBC drama, old girl. We were fed on it as kids. Jolly fine fare, too, I say, old bean!"

"At school, we actually called each other 'old bean'. Can you believe it?"

"You're kidding me, Sahara. I thought that lingo was reserved for BBC telly and upper-crust do's. Not real life."

Now it's Sahara's turn to strut. She leans back, thrusting out her pelvis, pretending to smoke a cigar and imitates one old bean talking to another. In minutes, she has Cowrie bent double, weeping with laughter at the absurdity of the scene.

"But didn't you go to a British girls' school? You know, great breeding grounds for horsey-faced society ladies and dykes."

Sahara grins. "No. I got lucky. My mother's brother ran a boys' prep school. When mother left, he knew Dad had no money for our education, so he offered to take me and my brothers for free. We stayed there during the week and went home on the weekends."

"But how did you survive in that environment as a girl?"

"My hair was cropped short like the boys and because Uncle Quentin ran the school, everyone accepted us. I even made it to the first eleven."

Cowrie's eyes widen. She checks Sahara's expression carefully. "You're not having me on are you?"

Sahara reaches into her wallet and extracts some photos. One shows her dressed in a choir outfit, which she explains is a cassock, with a white tie at her chin. In another, she sits plumb in the middle of the cricket team. Cowrie is speechless. Sahara takes full advantage of the moment and bursts into a boy soprano rendition of the "Allegri Miserere" solo. Her voice is exquisite, touches her listener deeply. After she's finished, Cowrie swears she sees an angel hovering above the nikau palm fronds, her wings shimmering in the heat.

"Mahalo, Sahara. Now that's a part of your tradition that really moves me. Gothic cathedrals and boy sopranos could even lure me into the coloniser's land to have a closer look."

"Glad to hear it, Cowrie. So you'll visit me after I return home?"

"Only if you sing to me like an angel."

"I'd be delighted."

Irihapeti interrupts their moment of intimacy to tell them to meet at the marae kihini to get water and kai for the trip. They finish packing and head for the community kitchen, swapping stories of their schooldays.

Ma roto hoki kia ora ka pai te korero.
If the inner person is refreshed, the conversation will
be agreeable.

After galloping up the coast for a mile, they head inland,
to the heart of the dunes. Far from being a city slicker,
Sahara is an expert horsewoman, having ridden for her
team at school. She admits she'd not gone bareback
before, but soon adjusts. Once they move into the softer
dunes, it's clear why they need to be on horses. It would
take hours to make progress on foot. When they stop for
lunch, they sink knee deep into the sand. Kuini suggests
they remount and head for the stream that runs down to
the sea so the horses can have a drink too. Here, there is
shade under a few scraggy manuka. In the distance,
dunes as far as the eye can see.

"Have you ever been lost in here?" asks Sahara.
"There's so few landmarks and the dunes all look alike."

"To the untrained eye they might, but unless there's a
sandstorm, you can usually follow your tracks back to
the sea, then you just ride along the coast," explains
Irihapeti.

Sahara looks over to the far dunes. Wind has created
ripples of sand that mimic ocean waves as they roll in
toward them. In the distance, mighty dunes, each one
higher than the former, layering the landscape. They can
no longer see or hear the ocean, and the dry desert
engulfs them; the only relief is the trickle of stream that
flows from the far mountains and out to sea. She screws
up her face as heat shimmers from the grainy surface,

trying to imagine her parents making love in the sand. How could she have been conceived in such arid conditions? Yet the magic of the dunes her mother recounted to her is apparent even here in this foreign land. Mountains of hope. That's how her mother described them. Before she abandoned her and her brothers. They'd never heard from her except for brief snatches of information from Uncle Quentin. Evidently, she was staying in some mansion and teaching English as a foreign language in France. Beyond that, she knew nothing. At least she has this in common with Cowrie, whose mother also deserted her, leaving her at the local orphanage. One night they shared stories in the hut, but it brought up more pain than relief for Sahara and she was glad when Cowrie dropped the subject.

"Hey, Sahara. Come and help me make a fire for the billy." Cowrie is collecting twigs from beneath the manuka. Sahara joins her while Kuini and Iri unpack fruit and dried smoked kahawai. They grub amongst the leaves and twigs for suitable fire material. Suddenly Sahara screams, flinging her hand and arm around wildly. "Oh, my God. It's the ugliest looking giant cricket I've ever seen. Get it off me!"

"Ok, Sahara. Just hold your hand still. It's scared. It won't hurt you. It's not poisonous."

Sahara gapes as she tries to hold her hand steady. The cricket's claws are barbed and dig deep into her skin. "Poor bugger. It's clinging on for dear life," remarks Kuini. "Now look closely, Sahara. Isn't she so beautiful? Look at the barbed feet and scaly back, those gorgeous prehistoric jaws, those exquisitely long antennae. She's a female bush weta. They're a protected species in Aotearoa and it is a privilege that she chose you to cling to."

Sahara is too frightened to move and Cowrie doesn't get very close either. "Well, I hope it's my last encounter with one too, Kuini. You're sure it won't bite?"

"Yep. We don't have any poisonous bugs or snakes in Aotearoa. That's why they call us the clean green Paradise. But don't tell too many Poms. We've got enough crawling over the country as it is." Sahara looks up to see if Kuini is joking or serious. It's impossible to tell. She glances back down to the weta. Its body is the colour of kauri and it is an impressive-looking creature. Kuini holds her hand next to Sahara's so the insect can crawl over. She gently places it onto a tree branch. "There. Now count yourself lucky you didn't encounter our ancestors or we'd've eaten you for lunch." She grins and returns to face the others. Sahara is pale but relieved the creature is not so close. She can now admire it from a safe distance.

"Did you really eat them?" she asks. "Barbs and all?"

"Yeah, the legs crisp up nice, finger licken good," adds Iri, with just the flash of a grin. Sahara joins their laughter.

Kuini bends to reveal a nest of huhu grubs at the foot of a tree. "Hey, Sahara. Have a squizzy here. Now these little beauties, as far as I know, are not protected like the weta—yet. So we'll have them for our entree."

"Now you really are kidding me!" exclaims Sahara. "I'm not that gullible!" She watches, horrified, as Kuini gathers up the huhu grubs, bites off their heads, cracking their bodies with her teeth, then places them on the lid of the coffee tin to roast over the fire. "Ugh, I have no intention of trying that!"

"Wasn't it the Poms who invented chocolate-coated grasshoppers?" jokes Iri. "The upper classes bought them from Harrods and served them up with a giggle at their cocktail parties as a bit of a lark."

Somewhere deep inside her memory, something stirs. "Oh, my God, Iri. You're right," admits Sahara. "I recall Uncle Quentin having guests to dinner one night. Some sort of weird collecting club. I remember it so well because they were all dressed the same. They looked like, how can I put it, like potato amphibians, with their pudgy wee bodies and their checks and ties." The three of them scream with joy at the description, and, on a roll, Sahara continues: "Uncle Quentin was a bit of an eccentric himself and he decided to shock them this night so he served up some sort of insect out of dainty little tins as if it was an exotic delicacy. They didn't know what to do. In British culture, it's important not to offend your host, especially when he is the headmaster of the local prep school all their sons go to. So they ate them, grimacing quietly and trying to be polite. Crispin and I were standing in the kitchen, looking through the leadlights. We thought we'd die trying to keep straight faces."

"Ok, Sahara! You are one helluva great storyteller. That gives you honorary status as one of us. I promise not to treat you like a Pom from now on!" Iri hugs her with delight. The others agree it's time to lay off the teasing.

"And I promise to at least try one of those hoohoo bugs."

Once golden brown, the grubs split open to reveal soft flesh and they taste the delight, imagining serving them up at an English cocktail party. "Hey, Sahara, you'd better take some home for Uncle Quentin. He'll be in his element!"

"Yes, I will. I wouldn't mind serving them up to him!" They follow the grilled beetle grub with smoked kahawai and fresh fruit. "A feast in the desert! What a treat! Thank you for bringing me here."

"Thanks for being such a good sport and taking the brunt of our jokes, Sahara. We do like you, ya know. It's just that we also enjoy having a scapegoat for the British colonialism that was forced on us at school. It's not personal."

"Yeah, just like we don't hate the French. We know many of them are against the tests too."

They fill themselves with talk, laughter and food, then mount their horses for the ride back. Once they've reached the beach, Kuini and Cowrie dive into the breakers while Sahara watches Irihapeti take out the fishing line she'd packed.

"Ok, Sahara, find me some stalks of toetoe and I'll teach you to fly."

"What's toytoy?"

"See that bush over there with the tall stalks of feathery plumage?"

"Oh, you mean pampas grass? Sure." Returning with the stalks, Sahara watches as the others, fresh from their swim, make a triangle with the sticks, tying the ends together with flax. They then weave raupo leaves over the frame, add paua shell eyes and leave two toetoe feathers dangling out the rear. Sahara, seeing a strange and wonderful kite emerging from their skilled hands, passes the fishing line to attach the string.

The wind is not strong enough for the kite to fly on their first run down the beach, so Sahara offers to take it on a gallop up the sand on her horse. She screams as she lets go of the kite, watching it scoop into the air and be carried on a gust of wind out to sea. Cowrie holds the string attached to a piece of driftwood, leaning back as the manu toetoe soars and swoops on reaching the wilder sea squalls. As Sahara releases the kite, Cowrie feels a fiery energy surge from the toetoe down the fishing line to her fingers, sizzle up her arms and through her body. She watches Sahara race down the beach. There's more to her than meets the eye. An invisible thread connects them which she does not fully understand yet.

Tangaroa, God of the Sea, can observe all that we are doing...

Tangaroa pukanohi nui.
Tangaroa, the God of the Sea, can observe all we
are doing.

Tension rises over the next few weeks as France
announces it will conduct eight underground nuclear
explosions in the South Pacific ending in March 1996.
The growing Peace Flotilla is determined that they will
prevent the tests by creating a global outcry. According
to Greenpeace, support is mounting in Europe and everyone is prepared for the protest to get ugly if the French
persist in testing against world opinion. Te Kotuku
Marae has become the headquarters for protest action,
and faxes, email and letters of support are flowing in
from all over Aotearoa. Kuini's workers at Te Aroha
have established an office for their activities.

"Hey, Sahara, listen to this." Cowrie balances on her
toes amidst a huge pile of letters. She holds one up to the
light. "This is from a group of school kids on Stewart
Island at the southern tip of Aotearoa. 'Tena Koe—We
live on an island like the Tahitians do. We like to fish and
swim and eat kai moana. If France tests under the water
at Moruroa, then radiation will leak out to all our
shores. We are sending our support to the islanders. Tell
the French to test their bombs in Paris if they are so safe.'
—Signed by twenty-two children."

"I've got one Maata brought in," adds Irihapeti. "It's
written by the kids here at the kohanga, in Maori and in
English. 'Dear Mr. Chirac. Some time ago, a local
fisherman created underwater explosions to kill fish to

eat. He thought it would be easier than fishing with a line. He killed our friendly dolphin, Opo. Children from all over our islands cried for weeks. Opo was a symbol of hope and love between all creatures on this earth. In addition, none of the fish exploded could be eaten, so it was wasted energy. They were split apart and got infected. They polluted our shores. Why are you doing this to innocent islanders in Tahiti? They are our brothers and sisters. Like us, they need clean water and fresh fish to survive. Please write back and tell us why you are doing this—Signed Maata, Piripi, Mattiu, etc.' "

"Would it be all right to reprint some of these letters in the UK press, Cowrie?" asks Sahara. "Of all the letters, it's the ones from children that really reach people at a heart level."

"That's fine. These letters are for the media and many have asked that we send them out. Greenpeace has hundreds more you could access. Hey, this bumper sticker is an old one from the Cold War: You can't hug your children with nuclear arms. And we thought we'd seen the end of nuclear testing and the arms race back then! This is so depressing."

"C'mon Cowrie. We need stronger fighting spirit than that. Where's your warrior self? This is gonna be a long battle and we need to keep spirits up. We've only just begun." Kuini puts the kettle on the gas ring, sensing it's time for a cuppa.

"Mahalo, Kuini. You're right. I'll make us a manuka brew." Cowrie walks outside the makeshift office and breaks a leafy twig off the nearest manuka, returns and places it in the pot. Sahara joins her at the bench and touches her lightly on the arm to show her support. A lightning charge enters Cowrie's body, re-energising her in seconds. She turns to Sahara, shocked at the power of her touch. But by now, the Brit has moved to reach for the bickie jar, seemingly unaware of her effect on Cowrie.

Later that night, after a long walk up the beach, they lie side by side in the dunes looking up at the stars. Sahara knows all the constellations but has not seen the Southern Cross from this aspect before. "Wow! It looks like a kite! There's the tip, the two wings and the tail with stars floating out like a banner as she flies. Imagine making a kite from the stars with the whole sky as your canvas." She sweeps her arm through the air. Cowrie sees a brush in her fingertips, dazzling stars coming out from her body and shooting into the stark sky to form the outline of a kite. "This one will have toetoe feathers to brush across the black canvas, and out of the feathers come new stars. See." Sahara arcs her arm over the sky and punches notches in the night air to indicate the birth of each shape she is creating.

Cowrie is entranced by her magic. "Ok, Sahara, this one's for you." She draws a feather starfish with tentacles flowing out from her body and reaching far into the distant skies.

Sahara smiles. "It's a Catherine wheel exploding into the night and sending her silvery shards across the galaxy oceans."

Cowrie gulps. This woman's imagination is wild, exquisite. "Nearly right. Now think of your image under the water, deep in the Antarctic, floating below gigantic icebergs, lighting the dark sea."

There is a breathless silence. Then, "She's a sea anemone, waiting for the perfect wave to burst her flower open to dazzle the seals."

"I think the sea anemone is you, sweet Sah. My sky painting is a feather starfish floating in the current,

66

swirling her sensitive tentacles like feathers, picking up messages from all over the planet."

"I'd like to be a feather starfish, then. That's my role down here. To hear the messages and transmit them accurately into the northern galaxy. Do you think my tentacles are sensitive enough?" She flutters her fingers, dancing them into the moist air. A cobalt wave surges up the beach and enters Cowrie's body, sweet salty water touching every cell, wetting her insides, flowing out her fingertips and toes. She takes a deep breath then holds her fingertips up to the tentacles so that they just touch, softly. She presses, releasing an energy that surges through Sahara. "Wow! If that's your answer, I like it." Sahara jumps up and rolls down the dune, turning cart-wheels along the beach below, energised by their contact.

Cowrie is breathless, her hand still suspended in the air. Her eyes follow the young Brit as her athletic body gracefully whirls over the sand. A moment longer and she'd have been tempted to kiss her. Did she know this? Did she break the moment of intimacy to avoid further closeness, or because the energy sparked her into move-ment? Cowrie rolls over on her belly to watch the action, her own body sensual and flowing. A couple of torea, digging for shellfish, scatter into the sky as a human wheel splashes past them on her flight up the beach. Cowrie laughs at their startled exit. She jumps up, flicks off her lavalava and runs down into the waiting ocean.

The moon reflects dazzling particles, like luminous starfish floating on the surface. The waves are large and inviting. She dives through the first one, surfs over the next and strokes out into the dark water. Once beyond the breakers, she glances back to shore to see if Sahara is ok. Now upright, she waves back. Cowrie beckons her into the water. Sahara edges close to the sea, but does not enter. Cowrie flips over onto her back, floats, looking up to the stars. Maybe she has a lover back home. Strange that she's never said. We connect so well, but maybe she just wants to be friends. That's cool. But the energy beween us is so electric. Perhaps I'll just have to be courageous and ask her. After stargazing a while longer, she's drifted further out to sea. She turns onto her belly and fins her way back to shore, coasting on the waves.

Sahara approaches the water, noting how like a sea creature her new friend is. She can't quite place which one, perhaps a seal surfing the waves? She's always been afraid of large waves, but didn't want to tell Cowrie this. She'd love to throw off her shorts and be able to enter the ocean like that, surf the waves as if she belonged in them. But she had been raised inland and not seen the ocean until her late teens. Once a child nearly drowned in a pool and it had taken all her courage to dive in and rescue her. But she was shaken afterwards. And the pool, thankfully, did not have waves. Yet a part of her longed to dive into the belly of a sea curve, swim into the core of danger, feel its embrace and stroke out beyond. The next wave carries the strange sea creature right up to Sahara's feet in the shallows. Looking down upon her rounded body with fins outstretched, it dawns on her. "Turtle! You look like a turtle from here," she giggles. Cowrie noses her feet, nibbling her toes. She screams like a child in delight. Each time she moves, the turtle nudges her ankles, tempting her into the water. They end up splash-ing each other until they are both thoroughly wet.

"Let's walk back to the hut and light a fire to warm ourselves. We can boil up some ginger tea." Cowrie is beginning to shiver in the night air after her time in the water. Sahara agrees and they make their way back over the dunes.

Sipping tea beside the fire, sharing stories of their youth, Cowrie raises the courage to ask Sahara why she ran off to do cartwheels at such an intimate moment of sharing, why she did not come swimming. Sahara takes a deep breath. "It's true, Cowrie. I've been avoiding this moment. I like you very much. I enjoy our closeness. But from the very beginning I sensed you were attracted to me and I've had to hold myself away because I'm not gay."

Cowrie sighs. Not again. First Koana, now Sahara. How could she be so naive? Sahara continues. "By that, I don't mean I'm only heterosexual. I don't believe in such strict gender lines. One day I'd like to be with a woman. I just know I am not ready for that yet. It's not a personal rejection. Just where I'm at currently."

"How come you didn't let on earlier? I'm so embarrassed I made such an assumption."

"That's ok. I wanted to tell you earlier but felt too shy."

"So how come your email address is Sappho at Island? I mean, that's a surefire hint."

"Oh, that's the local café. They have e-mail, faxes and access to the internet—so we all use it for our overseas messages. It is run by lesbians, true!"

Cowrie blushes, then laughs. "If you could've seen the way Iri and Kuini teased me about you wanting to come over and find a South Pacific lover, you'd've died! I hope this isn't going to get in the way of our work together."

"No! Nor our ability to have fun! I really love your energy, Cowrie, and I want us to be friends."

"So—do you have a boyfriend back home?"

"No—the last one was a cattle rancher in the Australian outback when I was covering the drought, and you definitely don't want to know that story."

"Was he that awful?"

"One day I'll tell you, but not now." A tear emerges in the corner of her eye and rolls over her cheek, dropping onto the soft earth. Cowrie is moved, wonders what pain lies beneath this tale, longs to hug her friend in comfort, but does not want her closeness to be misinterpreted.

"Another cuppa, Sah?"

"Ta." She reaches her arm over the fire for Cowrie to top up her cup, stumbles then screams in pain. The fire has seared her skin. Her cup crashes onto the burning manuka. The nearest cold water is at Mere's cottage, too far to help. Cowrie dashes into her hut and grabs the piece of kauri gum that acts as a paperweight. She takes out her fish knife, scrapes off some gum, mixes it with the manuka oil next to her bed, then applies the mixture directly onto Sahara's arm. She winces as the mixture touches her singed skin. But soon the ancient Maori herbal remedy starts soothing the pain. "Thanks, Cowrie. I shouldn't have been so careless."

"S'ok, Sah. You gotta take risks sometime." Cowrie smiles.

Sahara, sensing her meaning, replies "Yes. But I'm not ready to right now. I have some healing to do."

"You sure do, Sah. That'll take about a week to heal. Here, let me bandage it." Cowrie cuts two large leaves from the banana palm nearby and tears them into strips. She winds the fronds around her friend's arm gently, making sure she does not disturb the healing potion. Giant tears well behind Sahara's eyes, then pour out over her cheeks. She tries to wipe them away with her banana leaf arm, but realises it will hurt too much. She raises her other hand. Cowrie takes it in her own. "Just cry, Sah. Let it all out. It's good for you."

Sahara's voice is stilted as she gasps for breath

between her words. "It's more than you realise. The flame is symbolic. Remembering him brought it all back. That poor charred creature. I'll never forget. It stays in my mind like a nightmare."

"Maybe talking about it will help?" offers Cowrie.

Sahara hesitates a moment then speaks slowly. At first she had fun with the cattle rancher. But one night he got his Aboriginal servants to pack them a meal and ride out at dusk to the edge of the last remaining bush on the farm. He ordered them to light fires around the perimeter and grabbed Sahara, ripping off her clothes, saying how sexy it was to make love beside an inferno. She tried to resist. He raped her in front of them all while the bush blazed—then ordered one of his "natives" to take her back to the house. He didn't seem interested in her after his conquest. She stayed awake all night, shivering in the heat. The next morning, he was gone. But one of the boys brought back the furless body of a charred shivering koala who had been trapped in the flames. She felt as if she were inside the animal's pain and wept as she touched its raw charcoal paws.

"Ever since, I wondered how many other animals and birds got burned that night. It has put me off sex for a long time."

Tears have now wet Sahara's shirt. Cowrie wraps a warm blanket around her friend and holds her close, crooning waiata softly in her ear to ward off the nightmares. After a while, she is breathing deeply, far away in sleep. Cowrie searches her face, so dreamingly gentle, so soft. Her long lashes and full lips, her beautiful, perfect ears. She wouldn't be surprised to see wings sprout from her shoulders.

71

Mau ano te tinana, maku te ata o te tapara kau atu e.
For you the reality, for me only the shadow of desire.

Every day Cowrie dresses the burn on Sahara's arm, alternating between the kauri gum concoction and fresh manuka resin from the trees outside their hut. It is healing well. Lucky she can continue her work on her battery-driven laptop. Sahara walks to the marae media centre daily and checks out the latest developments, then writes up her stories, consulting with Kuini and Cowrie over certain details to make sure the cultural context is accurate.

Only one more week until the first Peace Flotilla boats leave. Tension is high and the elders are still debating whether women should be allowed to paddle the ancestral waka around the test zone. It flies in the face of tradition. Kuini reckons it's more heterosexual conditioning. After all, the waka and its paddler are supposed to represent the act of sexual union between man and woman. The symbolism goes back to ancient waiata. So, she reasons, what would it mean if a woman was stroking the waters? Sexual union from woman to woman? But no—we can't possibly admit that—even though some of the women singers of those waiata sleep together. Heated discussion ensues which is never resolved.

Cowrie is in charge of stocking the pantry and cooking on board the trawler. They've agreed to let Sahara travel with them as far as Tahiti—but whether she stays on board or covers the action from shore is yet to be decided. Today, they are all pitching in to give the boat her final coat of paint for the new journey. Finally the *Manawa Toa* is ready for action. By now, Sahara's burn has faded and she can use her arm. She keeps the banana leaf bandage on to protect it from dirt and being infected and asks Cowrie to make sure she packs some manuka resin and kauri gum for the trip—just in case.

All week, when she visits the media office, Kuini teases her about her concern for Sahara and the growing closeness she sees emerging between them. Finally Cowrie silences her taunts by telling her Sahara is heterosexual, though Kuini refuses to believe it. When she sees Cowrie isn't joking, she commiserates: "Some of my best friends are het, Cowrie. And anyway, since when did you let that stop you? Where's your sense of adventure?"

"Don't tease me, Kuini. I've really fallen for this special woman. There's something soulful in our connection that goes beyond all boundaries and I want to explore it. Please don't hassle us. Let her find her own identity in her own time. Meanwhile, I'm still trying to figure out how on earth I missed all the signals."

"Maybe she wasn't very clear with them?"

"Maybe. But she apologised for taking her time telling me. She didn't mean to lead me on. It's just that sensuality flows so easily from her. It's her vibrant life connection. She isn't even fully aware of it herself yet. I find her approach to life fascinating and refreshing. We've shared many stories of our childhood and there's so much connection, even though we come from utterly opposing traditions. That's a part of what makes it so interesting. We're all about to share a powerful experience sailing up to the test zone—and it's vital we work together as a team. I don't want divisions emerging that will tear us

73

apart. The work we're setting out to do is far too important."

"I agree with you on that, Cowrie. Enough said. I just feel so sad. You are an unusual but stunning team. It's surprised me too. I was suspicious of her motives at first, simply because of her background, but I like her now. I just wish you'd finally meet your match."

"Maybe I have. But she's just come in a form that was totally unexpected."

"Perhaps. But tread carefully, Cowrie. I don't want to see you as hurt as you were over Peta. How is she by the way? It's ages since I've asked after your US friends."

Cowrie smiles. Her former lover is now partners with an old college mate, Nanduye, and they work for land rights on the Kahnawake reservation in Canada. The break-up had been painful. But they'd mended the rift, healed well through the journey. "She's great, actually. I do miss her. She and Nan are currently touring reservations throughout the US and Canada, preparing a book on land rights."

"What about that crazy queer Benny and the crew at Grove Street?"

"Benny is filming 'earth power energy sites', travelling the States on her BMW with a Lady Di lookalike in leather. The Grove Street Gang have a new flatmate downstairs in my old apartment—from Aussie. Turns out she's a pretty hard case and keeping up the pressure from the south on my behalf. Squish suspects she's an ex-lover of Benny. Her name's Lizard. And Siliyik, the performance group, are doing gigs down the West Coast. I get regular postcards from Uretsete and DK updating me on events. They usually give two entirely different stories, but between them, I get the general idea. DK is given to hyperbole from time to time."

"Not unlike someone else I know, eh? No wonder you two get on so famously."

"Hey Cowrie," yells Iri from the far desk. "An email from Koana. Says she'll see you in Tahiti. The Kanaka Maoli movement are sending a support team to help organise land-based marches in Fa'a'a and Pape'ete. Mauva sends her love also and wants to know the date of your arrival."

"Email her the latest details. Thanks Iri. I'm going back to the hut to see how Sah is."

After she leaves, Kuini walks to the desk. "I'm worried about Cowrie. If she falls in love with this het—she's in for a deeply painful time."

"You can't stop her, Kuini. Anyway, I'd say it's too late. They fire each other's imaginations. They'll find a way to express this. Loving does not always have to be split down strict gender lines. After all, I came out with a married Rarotongan church woman, remember? Who'd've imagined that?"

Kuini laughs. "True! I don't understand you youngies. It was much clearer in the good old days of lesbian feminism, before queer culture even had a name."

"Yeah—but dykes have always been around. They may not have had a name for Sappho but they knew about her loving, enough to want to destroy her poetry. Besides, who knows with Sahara? She's not afraid to hang out with dykes, clearly. Or to cross over cultural boundaries. She's quite a risk-taker. Imagine leaving England for Te Kotuku Marae!"

"She probably didn't know what the hell she was coming to."

"Yeah—but she's coped pretty well. And we did give her a helluva hard time for the first few weeks, eh? I reckon we should just leave them to it."

"Reckon you're right. I just can't keep my sticky beak out, eh?"

"Cause you love Cowrie so much, Kuini. I know that. Sometimes wonder why you two never got it together. I used to think you would."

"Get away! We're too bloody similar."

"Just my point. It's the differences that attract Sahara and Cowrie to each other. It's for them to see which they can bridge and which they can't. You cannot protect them from pain. It'll happen anyway. But there's clearly enough joy to make it worthwhile."

"Maybe you're right. Ok. Let's drop it. What's the latest on the long-range forecast? Reckon we'll miss the tropical cyclones en route to Tahiti?"

"It's closer to the typhoon season. There could be some trouble. But we have to risk it, Piripi says. At least we'll get to shelter at Rarotonga on the way."

"So you can check out the local talent, eh, Iri?"

"You're incorrigible, Kuini. Go and see how progress on *Manawa Toa* is going and report back before dinner."

"Aye aye, captin." Kuini salutes her and saunters off to the harbour.

He pukai to Tu, he pukai to Rongo.
A heap of war, a heap of peace.

Most of the Hokianga region has turned up to farewell the *Manawa Toa* crew. Representatives from several Tai Tokerau iwi join together to bless the boat with karakia. Garlands and lei of bougainvillea, pukapuka and fern leaves crown their heads and the farewell waiata is sung by Maori and Pakeha alike. Intermarriage in the Hokianga has bred a fascinating mixture of people who, by and large, respect each other's differences. Native hibiscus flowers decorate the *Manawa Toa*, which looks resplendent with her green, cream and maroon markings. A koru sits below her new prow carving, depicting a dolphin splashing from the water in freedom, the waves swirling at her tail like fiddlehead ferns unravelling in pride. Along an entire side of the deck and beyond her tail is the mighty carved waka which will be released into the water to symbolically encircle the test zone, reminding the world this atoll belongs to the South Pacific nations, who will not rape her by penetrating her body with gigantic drills nor fill her with explosives of a higher detonation than Hiroshima.

The occasion is both solemn and celebratory. Speeches in Maori and English reflect the determination to carry the struggle for independence in the Pacific and the indisputable link between colonisation and nuclear testing to the world's media. Sahara tapes the proceedings so she can get Kuini to translate them for her and transmit their essence to the northern hemisphere. An independent telecommunications network has installed the latest technology onto the boat so that the news can be conveyed as it occurs.

Tradition prevailed in the debate over the waka crew. A full contingent of iwi men volunteered, and it was decided that the women's roles as communicators of news and in overseeing the wellbeing of the crew were just as vital. Piripi whispered to Kuini, however, that if any of the men got ill, Kuini, Cowrie and Iri would have to take their places. Kuini, grinning, murmured to Cowrie that she might think about spiking the food one night with a semi-harmful seaweed, like desmarestia, which would cause a bit of vomiting and diarrhoea, but even Cowrie admitted she would not descend that low. Besides, as she suggested, the weed turns bilious green after reaping from the sea and would probably be unpalatable. And none of them knew if it flourished in the warmer Tahitian waters.

But today, all such debates have been put aside. The crew have vowed to remain united in their cause. As farewell waiata are sung and the boat begins pulling out from the Opononi pier, men line the beach and deliver a powerful haka—a challenge to the crew and world to bring peace back to the Pacific or be prepared for the consequences of the rape of the land. Smaller waka, kayaks, rafts and other craft follow the *Manawa Toa* to the Hokianga Heads. In a final gesture of defiance and support, they raise their paddles to the heavens. The last karakia echoes back on the wind.

Waves breaking over the Hokianga Heads bear testament to all the foreign sailing vessels which have dared to enter the port, swirling over ghostly graves of sunken material assets and alien skeletons. On board *Manawa*

Toa, the kuia chant to invoke their ancestors for protection, to lay the sunken graves to rest. They clear the heads safely and begin steaming up the Tasman Sea toward the tempestuous waters where it meets with the mighty Pacific at the tip of Cape Reinga.

The inevitable seasickness is treated with native herbs administered by kuia. Sahara fares better than Cowrie or Kuini on this score, her body adapting to the motion well. "Must be the voyager in you, Sah. Maybe Captain Cook was a relly," suggests Cowrie.

"I don't think so. But I remember seeing his statue as a child. I thought he was a brave pioneer."

"We learned the same at school, Sah. The same fellas wrote our history books back then. It's not that he wasn't a pioneer. It's just that the books needed balancing so both sides of the story get out."

Cowrie is wanted in the galley so she disappears, leaving Kuini to translate the morning's speeches and karakia for Sahara's first media message to go out on the BBC's Alternative Radio. Halfway through their work, Kuini rushes portside to puke over the rail. Sahara joins her to make sure she is all right, wondering why she didn't run for the closest side. Kuini replies, with a sickly grin, that she couldn't defile the side of the boat the waka was on, and besides, this way the Aussies get the outfall. Sahara is about to note this on her pad when Kuini grabs it off her, threatening to chuck it in the sea. They laugh.

Life on board settles to a steady routine. As they round Cape Reinga, the old scow's sails are raised for the journey into the Pacific. The area of turbulence where the Tasman and Pacific oceans meet fascinates Sahara. She never thought it would be so visible, so powerful. As if a vast battle was being fought between the oceans. The white crests of the competing waves smash into each other, creating oceanic eruptions. Overhead, clouds threaten rain and an atmosphere of brooding turbulence casts shadows on the surrounding waters, deepening the dark jade waves with charcoal strokes. Jagged rocks spike the coastline and a sturdy cream lighthouse issues out of the mist on the headland. On a small rocky outcrop, a lone windswept pohutukawa survives. Kuini explains that this is the sacred tree where the spirits from dead bodies rest before flying out over the Pacific to their final destination in Hawai'iki. The kuia chant blessings and karakia as they sail past the pohutukawa.

Sahara leans over the starboard rail to take in the misty atmosphere, imagining a spirit soaring from the tree at dawn, floating over their heads on the flight north. She clutches the piece of kauri gum Cowrie gave her before she left to ensure a safe journey. Suddenly, the boat is hit by turbulence as the opposing waves battle it out for dominance, throwing the crew into each other and the rails. The golden rock flies out of her hand to be captured by the surging seaspray and drawn into its watery grasp. She watches, distraught, while the treasured resin sinks beneath the jade waters. As the boat tips back into balance, a soaring sense of elation rips through her body. The pain that resides in her burned left arm, and which has always invaded her left side at times of struggle, disappears, as if freed by the wave.

Later that night, snuggled in their hammocks on the deck, she tries to communicate the feeling to Cowrie. Her friend smiles knowingly. She explains that the moment the wave hit the boat they were equidistant between the sacred pohutukawa and Kapo Wairua, Spirit's Bay. That anything could happen in this spiritual realm. She'd heard wild stories from Tai Tokerau fishermen, including one where a huge fish tried to tow the boat out to sea. They had to cut the line to break free.

"But you gave me the kauri gum to ensure a safe journey—so does this mean I'm at risk now?"

"I don't know, Sahara. We're all at risk just attempting this voyage in the typhoon season, let alone what the French may do to us at the other end. But it's a risk we've agreed to take. The alternative is living in a contaminated Pacific—and that's too horrendous to contemplate not acting. Besides, it sounds as if the ocean claimed your place of pain. Maybe you need to learn to make that release, let go of it."

"Yes. I've been thinking about that all afternoon. The left side of the brain represents the logical side, doesn't it? The training of my education, family and career path. Maybe I need to follow my instinct more. Take risks?"

"Yeah, well you sure are by committing to this voyage, Sah. You're symbolically diving into the belly of the wave, even if you haven't worked up the courage to do it physically yet—so take it as a sign of courage. All the same, I'd take care to protect yourself on this journey. Be vigilant if we get caught up in action. You might be called on to test out your instinct in the midst of danger, so be prepared."

"Thanks, Cowrie. I will. I don't recall much about my mother, but I do remember her holding me as a baby and crooning into my ear. She told me in letters to the boarding school that I should always follow my heart instinct, never just do what others expect, or I'd end up being disappointed later. She was quite an activist in her time I think, in her own way. My father never forgot that side of her." Sahara gazes into the clouds, as if expecting to see her mother floating past and winking at her in approval.

82

"You should listen to her and draw on that strength, Sah. You might need it. Hey, can you hand over my shirt? It's on the mast hook just above your head."

"Here it is."

"Mahalo." Cowrie dips into her breast pocket and takes out a tiny cowrie shell. She holds it in her palm and closes her eyes, chanting a blessing into the shell, then passes it to Sahara. "Here. She will protect you. Now don't go throwing her over the deck!" She grins.

Sahara takes the shell, folding her fingers around its curved back. She opens her palm to reveal a beautiful creature with purple markings beneath the mottled brown spots of its shell. She rolls it over to notice a ridge of cream teeth where the shell folds in on herself, disappearing into its interior. "Thank you. I've never seen such a gorgeous shell. She has markings like a sea turtle. She reminds me of you."

"She's a cowrie shell and I was named after her by Apelahama, my grandfather."

"Wow! Cowrie is also an ancient word for vulva. Now I can see where it came from. Just look at this exquisite opening, almost inviting us in."

Cowrie cannot resist teasing Sahara. "You can enter her any time you wish. She holds mysterious power, secrets of the universe. It's like entering the wave. You have to do it to know what magic can be revealed from her hidden interior."

Sahara blushes, receiving her message on all levels intended. "Ah, but if I enter her, how will she remain a symbol of protection for me?"

Cowrie had not banked on having to answer for her suggestiveness. She plays for time. "She can hold you inside her folds of protective shell layers."

"But how would I breathe?"

"Through the opening of the vulva. Like this." Cowrie takes the shell and turns it on its side in Sahara's palm. "See, she's smiling." Sure enough, there is a huge grin the length of the shell face.

Sahara giggles. "Ok. I believe you. But for now, I think I'll just tuck her into my pillow and dream on her for protection. What will you have for safety now that you've given her to me?"

"Oh, she'll still protect me. I don't need her on my body. She's safe inside my soul. She was ready to be released."

"Thank you, Cowrie." Sahara blows her a kiss from her hammock and Cowrie catches it mid-air and places it firmly on her cheek, sliding it sensuously down to her lips. "You are so bad!" Sahara whispers, grinning. It does not bother her that Cowrie is openly seductive since she feels it's better out in the air than brewing beneath the surface. She'll get over her crush soon.

Cowrie lies on her back in the wind on the top deck, wondering if Sahara will open out more about her mother at some stage. She folds her hands under her head and looks up into the stars. The Southern Cross seems closer out here on the ocean, a dazzling kite lit by explosions of light. Astronomers say stars are self-luminous bodies. But what makes them shine so brightly at night? She hopes these are the only explosions they'll encounter, but deep within her belly, a pit of fear is opening, telling her that the battle ahead will be a tough one. She calms herself by letting the joy of this new friendship enter her and sends waves of aroha to the cowrie shell vibrating gently through the pillow under Sahara's head.

Ko Tahu kia roria.
Let the tapu be removed from Tahu.*

She soars through the night sky, her wings longing to touch the ocean waves below. From a tuft of floating seaweed, the muffled crying of a baby takapu caught in a fisherman's net. She dives down towards the waves, instinctively, knowing they could capture her in their wet clamp also, but following her motherly instinct. Nearing the mound, she sees a human child floating on a nest of human hair. It stops crying and smiles. Around the tuft of hair, in the shape of a topknot, are protective shells. She soars back on an updraft, knowing the child is protected, and continues her journey home to lay her eggs on the speckled windswept crag at Muriwai Beach, Aotearoa.

"You fellas hungry?" Kuini brings a pile of freshly caught kahawai, smoked over the barbecue, to rest in front of the scientists, activists and crew members. They rip into the thick cream and grey flesh with their hands, eager to taste kai moana again after a few days of abstinence enforced by the rough seas and nausea.

"Ka pai, Kuini. Mahalo." Cowrie removes the backbone of the fish and exposes the lower layer to the eager devourers.

"Enjoy it while you can," warns Piripi. "Last time I was on Maohi soil we could not eat from Maohi seas because most of the fish were contaminated."

*This is the whakarori ceremony which removes harmful influences from food and destroys tapu.

85

"But that was the early days of nuclear testing, eh bro? Times have changed since then."

"Not really. It's still risky. Heaps of reports of diarrhoea and vomiting and all sorts of shit, man. Your poo looks like green curry and ya chuck up for weeks if ya get that sea poisoning cigaretty shit."

"Ciguatera. That's the name for marine food poisoning, and yes, it is very serious and very common in Tahiti since the testing began," adds Henry, one of the Department of Conservation scientists. "It's especially so in the bigger fish that make up much of the Maohi diet, and French Polynesia has over six times the Pacific average of this disease, which cannot be related to anything other than the testing there."

"So how did the Frogs ever get so much power over these islands? I mean the Poms came and laid claim to Aotearoa and made us sign a treaty, then tricked us into believing they'd honour it. But how can you take over all those islands that make up Tahiti and retain control when they are so spread out and so diverse?" The Nga Puhi crew member screws up his face and sucks on a drag of wacky baccy, staring upwards, as if the heavens might answer him.

"Long story," answers Piripi. "Short stick is that the French wanted the islands for use of their whaling, war and trading boats, so they forced Queen Pomare IV and a few important chiefs to sign their so-called protectorate treaty—similar shit to te Tiriti o Waitangi—established a government to take over, and by the time the Poms heard about it they were pipped at the post."

"Bloody good lark. Could be the only decent thing the Frogs ever did—and that was to beat the Poms at their own game," chuckles one the of crew.

"Yeah, but not so funny when you see the devastation that resulted from their colonisation.

"Similar tactics were used for taking over Hawai'i. This is no coincidence." Cowrie rips a piece of flesh from the kahawai, wondering if it will make them bilious tonight.

"Same all over the Pacific," replies Piripi. "All over the world. You can't look at nuclear issues without looking at the history of colonisation here. They go hand in bloody hand. From nuking Moruroa to digging uranium from Aboriginal soils to ripping up Navajo and Hopi land for uranium at Big Mountain. It's the same game, and in every case it is whites nuking blacks."

"Now, now, old chap. That's a bit rough isn't it?" Albert, a pakeha from Southland radiology, lights his pipe and looks down the length of his considerable nose.

"Sure is, if you are on the receiving end," mutters Kuini.

Piripi takes in a deep breath and continues. "France has now circled the earth with its military bases, second only to the USA in the range of military hotspots outside their own countries, of course. Tahiti is the heart of all this action, right in the middle of the map, allowing them the ability to nuke anything anywhere and test their weapons as far away from global outrage as they can manage."

"He's right there," adds Albert, not wanting to alien-ate himself from the group. "I'll never forget de Gaulle's words announcing the nuclear testing site. He said, 'In order to thank French Polynesia for its faithful attach-ment to France I have decided to set up the Centre d'Expérimentation du Pacifique there.' Amazing langu-age for a test site."

"Well, Maohi protested en masse, and de Gaulle replied bombs would only be exploded when winds blew from the north across empty ocean between Polynesia and

Antarctica. Imagine that! Empty oceans between the Tahitian islands and the Antarctic. Forget Aotearoa or Aboriginal land." Piripi slams his hand on his thigh. "So testing began in '66, three years after the Yanks, Poms and Russians had agreed to limit detonations, and the first test was devastating. Reports emerged from Maohi who saw it that the explosion sucked water from the lagoon and covered the islands with contaminated dead fish, seaweed, junk, you name it. Two months later, de Gaulle visited and could not wait for the wind to change, some party in Paris it was said. Anyway, he demanded the test be held. Scientists monitoring the tests in Niue, Cook Islands, Samoa, Tonga, Tuvalu and Fiji said their instruments recorded massive radioactive fallout. Between '66 and '74 another forty-four detonations destroyed the land and sea around Moruroa and Faungataufa atolls, and serious birth defects were appearing in Maohi babies, many born dead. They were sent to France for further tests and disappeared. Many Maohi still do not know where their babies are and mourn them daily. Gradually fallout spread as far south as Aotearoa, though it's still denied by scientists dependent on French funding."

There is silence among the crew, all of whom recall relatives who have lost their kids to pakeha medicine or science, who heard stories about their island relatives but never knew the full implications of French military control of the Pacific.

"Shit. We could've become French-speaking clones if we hadn't've gone anti-nuke, eh bro?"

"Still could, Rewi," replies Piripi thoughtfully. "All the more reason for our solidarity now, bro." He touches Rewi's shoulder, remembering his grief when his first son was born with a degenerative bone disease, knowing the strontium fallout could have caused it in Tahiti.

Manawa Toa continues her journey. Each day they share talkstory and gradually the extent of French domination and the realisation that they are a part of something much larger and more insidious than nuclear testing in the Pacific dawns on them. Piripi stresses that this resistance is not just for Maohi or indigenous people of the Pacific, but for all who have signed treaties in good faith and been used as military or economic targets in return. That it is a holocaust of a different name, but again enacted in silence and oppression, where even those who know about it dare not speak out.

Sahara, who has taken notes throughout, is in a state of shock after they disperse. She fears for their safety and for that of the crew, now knowing this is not just a friendly protest as most of the media paint it to be. Much more is at stake here. Cowrie calms her, telling of her dream the night before of flying like a giant takapu, thinking she must rescue her chick from the deathly contaminated seaweed bed, then realising, on flying closer, it is a human baby, that of Maui-Potiki, the last-born child of Taranga. She explains that after Taranga gave birth to Maui, she thought he was dead, so she snipped off her topknot, coiled it around the body and floated it out to sea. Because the hair was from a tapu or sacred part of her body, it possessed protective powers, would take care of her floating child forever, just as they would be protected if they believed in the sacredness of their resistance and remained heart warriors to their cause.

He nui maunga e kore e taea te whakaneke, he nui ngaru moana ma te ihu o te waka e wahi.
A great mountain cannot be moved, a giant wave can be broken by the prow of the canoe.

The passage across the southern Pacific Ocean is turbulent and squally. Most of the crew have been sick. Messages from other boats in the Aotearoan Peace Flotilla bound for the test zone reveal that two have been caught in the tail of a typhoon. They refuel at Rarotonga, where they are greeted by a large contingent of Cook Islanders who provide a welcoming feast. The next stage of the journey is in rough seas, with only a lone albatross to keep them company. They sing waiata and offer karakia to Tangaroa, God of the Oceans, to ease the way.

By the time they reach the Tahitian Islands, the crew look forward to setting their feet on land. The waka survived the journey with only a few dents and bumps in the heaviest seas. A mile from the Pape'ete harbour, the canoe is lowered into the sea with paddlers aboard so they can enter the harbour in traditional style. Irihapeti radios through to Oscar Temaru, leader of the Tavini Huraatira, and Maohi are lining the shores to welcome them.

Sahara gasps at the awesome beauty of the towering pinnacles rising violently from the ocean below. She videos the entry into the harbour as the mighty waka leads them and is greeted by Tahitian canoes, outriggers, and a resounding haka from the shore. The harbour is dotted with craft guiding them in. As the waka reaches the shore, Tahitians move down the beach and shower the paddlers with bougainvillea, hibiscus and frangipani lei. The colours of the flowers shine in the brilliant sun. *Manawa Toa* ties up to the wharf and its crew are festooned with garlands and waiata.

That night, the speeches of welcome before the feast outline the gravity of the situation. Former workers from Moruroa Atoll, who had to sign a secrecy agreement in accepting their jobs with the French government to work at the nuclear test zone, risk their freedom by explaining how the military base works and the history of thirty years of nuclear explosions in the Pacific. They hand over diagrams of the nuclear plant which show extensive underground drilling has eroded several old test sites, and photographs which clearly indicate massive cracks in the surface of the atoll, visible from the water. Cowrie and the others have heard most of this before, but Sahara is shocked. "Little of this has filtered into the European media," she whispers, as the speeches continue.

"Who's going to make an enemy of France in the new economic union?" Cowrie replies. "Even if they knew this stuff, no government would risk peace with their neighbours for the sake of an island in the Pacific. You wait, I bet England doesn't denounce the tests. They're too close, with too much to lose."

Sahara is silent, listening to the next speakers who outline the colonial history. Over the years, the Maohi people have been exploited by France, England, Spain, the Netherlands, Chile, Peru and Russia. The one hundred and thirty islands of Tahiti, covering an area the size of Europe, have been subjected to colonial force and slavery, despite vigorous opposition. In 1797 the London Missionary Society sent a contingent of religious men to Tahiti but they were forced to move on to New South Wales. Then the French sent their missionaries. They wanted the islands to service their merchant, fighting and whaling boats. In 1842 they seized control, establishing a government. Then the Brits and French fought over the islands until 1843 when hundreds of French soldiers took Queen Pomare's palace by force, ripping down the Tahitian flag and raising the tricolour, which has presided ever since. Despite powerful Maohi resistance, they used material bribes and religion to take over the islands. Decades later, they established nuclear testing zones in return for schools and hospitals. In 1957, the islands became "French Polynesia".

Oscar Temaru, leader of Tavini Huraatira, continues the history. By 1962, de Gaulle proclaimed, without consultation, that the islands would be used as a nuclear testing site. Formerly, Fa'a'a had been a community of two thousand living off the rich resources of the land and sea. Suddenly they were invaded by the military. Then French civilians flooded in, lured by large wage packages and the prospect of living in Paradise. "The French tell us they are here to protect us. But we have no enemy! We are living in the Pacific! And that's what we want: to live peacefully in the Pacific. The French are doing their nuclear tests here to protect themselves, not us!"

The Aotearoan crew respond with waiata and tales of resistance from home, then food is offered. After the feasting, korero stretches long into the night. With bellies full of spit-roasted pork and juicy mangoes, Kuini, Iri, Cowrie and Sahara follow the shore line of Fa'a'a, leaving the negotiations for Piripi and the tacticians in the group to resolve. The warm night wind caresses their bodies beneath their lavalava.

"It's a matter of life and death, and everyone feasts as well as making speeches. This is so different from home."

"Who knows, Sah. What about your Irish ancestors?

Bet they feasted over the odd battle or two. Ate beef before battle and washed it down with honey mead or mulled wine."

"Whisky probably! Here, the connection to the earth, the land, seems to fire the spirit. Most of us have lost our ancient links to the land in the UK. Massive deforestation has robbed the earth of its power and made it arid and inhospitable. Hard to celebrate that."

"Yes—but imagine if Maohi believed the nuclear blasting had totally ruined their islands? They have more reason than most to be devastated, but they know the fight is still worth the effort. In your land, forests can be replanted, as is happening in Aotearoa where farmers raped the earth of its trees for their cattle."

Sahara is quiet as they walk. In the distance, the lights of Tahiti Fa'a'a airport gleam out from the shore. They debate issues raised by the speakers and discuss the huge task ahead. It looks as if France is determined to go ahead with the testing, no matter what form of protest takes place.

From the far trees, a muffled drumming. The airport fires, lit to guide the planes in, rage into the night sky, forming a mist over the land. As they draw closer, voices are heard above the usual drone of an airport. Suddenly, massive flames light up the sky and the crowd roars as the bonfire rages. Somewhere from behind, a police siren. They duck for cover under vegetation. "Shit! I think there's a riot going on," whispers Irihapeti.

"Good on them!" grunts Kuini. "Let's get closer."

"But if we get involved, we might be carted off to prison and then we'd be no use for the anti-nuke protest. You know how long the French have incarcerated Greenpeace protesters before. Could be weeks or months of negotiations."

"Yeah, or some sort of treason offence they'll manufacture. They're not likely to be lenient when the world's media are sleeping in the hotels of Pape'ete."

"Don't see too many media out here now."

"They probably don't even know it's happening. I mean, we thought the fires were to mark the tarmac."

"Sahara's here."

"Yes. I vote we go on. I need to cover this, especially if the other media remain tucked up in hotel beds. Who's with me?" asks Sahara.

They agree that Irihapeti should return to the boat to let Piripi know where they are, in case they get caught, and to make sure *Manawa Toa* does not leave without them. The others will go on. Sahara has a surprisingly fiery spirit for one so gentle. Maybe it's her media training. She is not afraid to lead them on even though she is least familiar with the territory. Kuini and Cowrie wink at each other behind her. "Imagine a Brit leading us into the war zone against colonial oppression, sis. Here's one for the books," Kuini whispers. Out loud, she urges Sahara on. "Go for it, sister!"

Sahara creeps through the undergrowth in front of them until they reach the edge of the tarmac. By now fires are raging over the airport base and the terminal is blazing. Police cars have driven out to protect the planes, and fire engines are desperately trying to quell the blaze. Riot police are violent when they grab the Tahitians. Many are beaten to the ground and others are rounded up for the prison trucks. The protesters flee in all directions, but in the background a powerful drumbeat urges them on.

Sahara rushes out into the fray to get photos of the action as Maohi light fires in drums on the tarmac and the police struggle to capture them. Cowrie feels a tug at her heart and prepares to make a dash as a cop grabs

Sahara's arm. Kuini pulls her back harshly. "Have you lost your mind? Our job is to prevent nuclear testing. We have allegiance to the iwi. If we get involved here, we won't help the Maohi cause, and we'll let down our brothers and sisters." Cowrie knows she's right but she can't bear to see Sahara hurt. There is a sickly crunch as police truncheons make contact with human flesh and screams are heard above the sound of the drums. Sahara is lost in the fray.

Crowds rush into the bush to disperse. Nearby, a group of three gendarmes bashes a young Tahitian boy until he is bruised all over. They leave him in a pool of blood. The protesters and police surge on. After they've moved closer to the terminal, Cowrie and Kuini drag the youth into the bushes and tend to his wounds. Turns out his name is Raoul and he was with his older brothers marching on Tahiti Fa'a'a airport. The organisers insisted it be the usual peaceful march but a few angry members said it was time to give up non-violent action and let the world know how badly they'd been treated. By the time they'd reached the airport, several other groups had joined the march, some armed with fire bombs. But it was only when a youth lit a fire inside a drum that the riot police swooped down on them. It was as if they were waiting in the wings for violence to erupt. Everyone got caught up in it then.

The boy looks about fourteen. His story emerges between gasps as they clean the blood with sea water and dress the wounds by tearing his lavalava into strips. Kuini asks where he lives as he'll never make it home alone. He is scared to move lest the police attack him again and put him in prison. His older brother was in a protest two years ago and he's still in police custody. He points in the direction of the hills behind Pape'ete.

"Hey, Cowrie. You got any cash? I reckon we'd get there faster by taxi and I know there's a stand outside the airport. Most of the drivers are Maohi, so we'll be safe."

Cowrie shakes her head. They try lifting the youth, but he cries out in pain. Could be internal. Just as they get him in an upright position, one arm slung over each of their shoulders, there's a rustle in the bushes. They freeze. A flashlight blinds their eyes. The boy struggles. Sahara bursts from the vegetation, her face and body covered in soot and a wound bleeding from her temple. Carefully, they lay Raoul down and attend to her, telling her never to leave the group again, or to at least tell them if she plans to take such a risk. Sahara apologises and explains she had to act on the spur of the moment. "Besides, I survived, camera intact." She holds up the beast gleefully.

"Sahara, we need to get Raoul home safely. Can we use your money to get a taxi? Are you strong enough to come with us?"

"Yes." Sahara adds, "I'm not so much hurt as exhausted." She slowly gets to her feet and Kuini indicates where the taxi rank is. "If you can nab a taxi, we'll bring Raoul."

"Ok." Sahara moves ahead and they follow.

Police and firemen are too busy trying to extinguish the fire in the terminal building to notice them. By the time they get to the taxi stand, Sahara is holding the car door open. The driver knows Raoul and takes them right to his home.

Te whare o te matata.
The home of the fernbird.

Raoul's mother invites them into the corrugated iron and palm leaf hut hidden in a community of similar make-shift homes not far behind the affluent main street of Pape'ete. They lay him on a woven mat and she cleans the wounds and applies papaya leaves to the bruises. Kuini suggests taking him to the hospital but she indicates it's not a good idea, that he'll be fine after resting. She wants to know what happened and gestures them to stay while she dresses the wound on Sahara's temple. They accept gratefully. They tell her what they know from Raoul and ask her about her family.

Her name is Toi and she explains Raoul is special because the three children before him all died, one from violent muscular contractions and one from leukemia. The third was malformed and died stillborn. Her husband, Jacques, died from cancer after working at Moruroa through the years of atmospheric nuclear tests. The hospital never confirmed the causes of death officially, although the nurses and doctors told her in each case. That was common practice. She'd been given a widow's pension for two years; then the terms of contract with the workers changed, many thought because of the high incidence of cancer-related deaths. Injured workers were flown to hospitals in France. But many never came back. She manages to convey this information in a mix of French, Tahitian and English.

Between them, they translate enough to understand.

Sahara asks Toi more questions in French, only some of which the others understand. Sadly, this is now her adopted language. Turns out her sister lived on Tureia Island, less than a hundred kilometres from Moruroa. The entire population, except for one man who refused, was removed to conduct tests there in '68. When they were returned, they were told not to eat fish or drink the water or grow crops on the land. It was contaminated. But how could they survive otherwise? Then there was her cousin who lived on Moruroa before testing began. The lagoon was a favourite fishing place. But only a couple of years after the blasts began in '66, the seafood was poisonous. People vomited and began to suffer all sorts of ailments. Now they live on canned food brought to the atoll.

It is now very late and they thank Toi and say they will check on Raoul before they leave. "Better you not come. They will ask questions. Too many questions." There is a look of pleading in her eyes. They agree to part here, and wish her well, saying they will do all they can to help stop the testing.

It is a short walk back to *Manawa Toa* and they make it in silence, not wanting to attract attention. It's nearly dawn and evidence of rioting in the township alerts them to the volatility of the situation. Broken shop windows are patched up with wood, and burned-out garbage cans litter the street. Signs telling the French to go back home and stop testing are pasted over shop facades, and a ripped banner of Chirac holding a malformed child with the words "*Meutre!*" beneath hangs between two power poles. As they reach the boat, a violent red sunrise appears on the horizon, deepened by smoke still hanging in the air. Like blood bursting from the water, spreading a cancer over the ocean. Their hearts are heavy and their bodies exhausted. After Sahara faxes in her report, they creep into their beds and sleep until they are woken by Irihapeti, who is relieved to see them safe.

A few hours later, with fresh supplies, Maohi paddlers and a French anti-nuclear scientist aboard, they slip anchor to sail to Moruroa. Only a handful of Tahitians are there to see them go. The mood is sombre and the sense of their mission is tense. Many witnessed the violent action of the riot police on the streets the night before and wonder how much further the French authorities will go to protect their most valuable asset at Moruroa. It is their entire defence system at stake. Suddenly, the issues become more complex, the danger more intense.

Cowrie wakes too late to cook breakfast but she is not let off the lunch shift. Preparing kai down in the galley, she asks the scientist, Marie-Louise, if the food is safe.

"*Oui*. Much of it is vacuum-packed and sent from France, which is why it's so expensive. Fresh fish is usually from islands at least a hundred kilometres from Moruroa. Most of the French eat imported food, so they're relatively safe. But Maohi have to rely on their local fresh supplies because they can't afford or don't want to eat the imported goods."

"How did you get involved in activism? I mean, as a French scientist, you'd be paid well to work for the military, I gather?"

"*Vrai*. I immigrated for the chance to escape to what the French government call 'Paradise'. Instead, I found a captive nation of Tahitians who'd been made dependent on us for their health and education. It's really bribery for ruining their islands with nuclear testing. Once the tests are finished, *c'est vrai*, they'll offer further bribes as compensation for a few years and then exit, leaving their nuclear waste plugged up behind shafts of concrete. The Americans did this in the Marshall Islands and the French will do it here."

Cowrie slices tomatoes and peppers for the salad, wondering where they come from. "So what made you stay and fight for change?"

Marie-Louise rests her arm on the table and sighs. "I fell in love with a Tahitian, Rua, and through him I got involved in the independence movement. At the time, I was still working on site at Moruroa and he was digging the shafts for underground testing. It was March '81 when we met. A hurricane blew radioactive waste which had been dumped on the west side of the atoll into the sea. We knew that hidden in the waste was plutonium from an accident in '79 that killed two of our technicians. There was major panic. The French government insisted that we hide all evidence of the damage and stay silent or we'd lose our jobs. That was the end of it for me. Rua's life was in danger. He was extracted from the shaft in the middle of the hurricane and very nearly didn't make it. I helped nurse him back to health. After that, we both decided to get jobs in Pape'ete and live with his family there."

"Did that work out?"

"Rua died three years later. Leukemia they said. Two of his brothers had died of cancer. Both worked at Moruroa. By then we'd become involved in the Maohi liberation movement and we provided them with plans of the test sites and all the knowledge we'd accumulated. After Rua's death, I was determined to keep fighting to end nuclear tests."

"Are you willing to release your information and experiences to the international media? We have a British

100

reporter on the boat who'd be very interested in your stories."

"Only if I can trust him not to release my name. The French authorities have ways of dealing with those of us who've worked inside and then shared information. Some have simply disappeared."

"I am absolutely sure you can trust her, but let's meet tomorrow, after you've had time to think about it, and see what you think of her."

"I'd be happy to do so. For Rua and for all the others."

"Have you ever suffered any side effects from working at Moruroa?"

"I have constant headaches and muscle cramps. My white blood cell level is higher than normal, but not in the danger zone. I've learned to live with it, like so many of us."

"All the more reason it must be exposed. How come the whole world has not heard these stories?"

"Many people fear the power of the French. We—no, they—are now in thick with Germany and together they rule Europe. England wouldn't dare question their nuclear power. They are an ally. With this facade of a united Europe, none of the smaller countries would dare either."

"Maybe they would if they knew what was really happening down here in the Pacific?"

"*Peut-être.*"

Piripi blows the conch shell to announce lunch and Marie-Louise offers to help serve. The food is laid out on tables folded down from the walls. An appetising and delicious feast. But Cowrie does not feel like eating today. She excuses herself after the karakia and climbs on deck for fresh air. Or is it fresh? Now she wonders about

101

everything surrounding them. They are heading for an atoll which the French declare is entirely safe. International scientists also declare it safe. But what about the stories of the people who live there, who rely upon the earth and sea to provide their food, who cannot afford and do not want to buy imported products?

Suddenly, she feels sick and rushes to the rail to vomit over the edge. Her bile is caught by seaweed floating on the surface, a dead fish enclosed in its watery grip.

He iti, he iti kahikatoa.
Though small, it is still a manuka tree.

Piripi discovers they got caught in the riot and repri-
mands them for their carelessness. Lucky he does not
know about Sahara's exploits. They agree they have
learned from the situation and that it's vital to work
together as a group, especially now they are entering
dangerous territory.

Sahara has spent most of the afternoon talking with
Marie-Louise. She joins Cowrie on deck after dinner.
"Delicious kai, thanks. I notice you haven't been eating
much lately. You still upset about Raoul?"

"Yeah—and his mother—and all the stories I've heard
from Marie-Louise since. Not sure if I want to eat any of
this food."

"At least you have a choice, Cowrie. Most of the
Tahitians don't."

"You're right, Sahara. I need to get a handle on this
grief or it will immobilise me. I guess the knowledge has
been floating around my brain, but it's in my body now.
It hurts."

"Remember that lecture you gave me about my
British colonial guilt shortly after I arrived in Aotearoa?
You said it didn't help to get caught in fear and shame.
You had to work it through and translate it into action."

"Yeah, reckon I did, eh?" Cowrie smiles weakly.

"Well, here's some action. I want you to check my
article about Marie-Louise. I've just drafted it and

anything can be changed. She's so brave to share this information. It's vital we get it out. Once you've ok'd it and she's checked the facts, Irihapeti will transmit it."

Cowrie takes the pages from her hands, pleased to be given a set task other than cooking food she suspects could have traces of contamination. They carefully sift through the material. Cowrie learns more. There is enough waste on Moruroa to fill 245,000 concrete containers, each holding 200 litres. Engineers from the Atomic Energy Commission wrote reports indicating that the atoll sank 1.5 metres between 1975 and 1981. The largest crack in the surface of the atoll is over 30 centimetres wide and 800 metres long, and radiation leakage has been detected ever since testing began but, according to government sources, is still under the allowable levels.

"Allowable levels? What does that mean? Some level made by scientists or measured by its effects on the local population? Sah, I think you should question it here. Go back to Marie-Louise and check that part."

"I agree. Thanks Cowrie."

Together, they examine the information for another hour and come up with a raft of questions for their guest. "Lucky she's here or we'd be really stuck."

"Yeah, I love it that she's French too. It's strongly subversive. Appeals to my sense of justice."

"I know. Hey Cowrie, I've been meaning to thank you for giving me this beautiful shell." Sahara presses the shape in her breast pocket. "I reckon that saved me from major harm in the riot. At one stage, a cop gripped my camera in one hand and raised his baton in the other. I imagined crushing him in my grip, the razor teeth of the shell cutting into him, and I knocked the baton out of his hand. He was so shocked he stepped back in disbelief.

The leather strap that held it to his hand was ripped in two with a jagged edge. It lay on the ground between us. Then I ran with the crowd. It was only later I remembered all the details. I was in still in a dazed state when I made my way back to where I'd left you and Kuini."

"You certainly shocked us with that camera flash. I was furious at the time."

"Sorry. It's the trained reporter in me. Knew I'd never get a shot like that again."

"Still got the film?"

"No. I gave it to Piripi to courier back to the UK when he went ashore for supplies. I may never see it again. I just trust my colleagues will know what to do with it. I inserted a note signing away syndicated media rights. I think I got some powerful shots of the police violence and terror in the eyes of the Tahitians."

"D'ya ever worry that you're exploiting a situation?"

"All the time. But the media, like it or not, play an important role in getting the information out. I didn't see any other reporters at Fa'a'a. No doubt by the time the riot reached the streets of Pape'ete they'd've woken up and documented it, but the airport riot was vital."

"Why should it be different from the street rioting?"

"Don't you see, Cowrie? It was an attempt to close the main system of transport, stop further journalists from entering Tahiti. Most members of the Maohi Independence Movement were with us feasting that night and from all accounts they've always resisted peacefully. Don't you think it's a possibility that the riot was incited by the authorities? How come so many were there at Tahiti Fa'a'a already decked out in their riot gear?"

"Whose side are you on?"

"Hey, settle down, Cowrie. I just want to get to the truth. Remember you told me Raoul said it was as if the gendarmes were waiting in the wings? It could've been staged. Maybe the idea was either to stop media attention or to grab media reaction to the violence. They like depicting the 'natives' as warriors, fighters, primitives who need civilising. These pictures could reinforce that or depict police violence, depending on their context. That's why I wanted the stories from Raoul's mother and Marie-Louise as well, to show the wider issues."

"D'ya really reckon the riots could have been incited by the authorities?"

"We'll probably never know. But it is possible."

Memories of burning drums and police batons flash through Cowrie's brain. It was like theatre, in the night, when the reporters were asleep so they did not see the action but would report the devastation the next day. In some ways, it made sense. Since many countries had condemned the resumption of tests, it was up to the French to get them back on side. One way would be to alienate people against the Tahitians. But surely it'd backfire in their faces? Too risky a stunt? Maybe they've underestimated what they're up against this time.

Sahara's hand brushes her cheek. "Don't worry Cowrie. We'll make sure the real stories get out there."

"Yeah, I know." Cowrie manages a smile. "Hey, I was worried about you in the riot, Sah. Kuini had to hold me back from joining you."

"She told me. She said you were like a bellowing elephant ready to rush out into the desert!" They laugh.

"You know when you said you felt the cowrie shell give you strength?"

"Yes."

"When that cop grabbed you, I flashed onto the shell in my mind."

"I'm not surprised. I felt like I had strength I never

knew about before. Now I believe that shells have a life of their own too."

"They do, Sah. Remember I told you about Hi'ilawe, born to Kakea and Kaholo, children of the cliffs, that night in the hut at Te Kotuku?"

"Yes, I remember."

"Well, I didn't finish the tale. She was abandoned by her mother, wrapped in moss and flung over a cliff. Hinauluohia finds the bundle containing the child and she sees it is of chiefly birth and since Pokahi, First Night, has been longing for a child, she brings her this beautiful girl Lau-ka-ieie. Pokahi and Kaukini raise her secretly with birds and flowers and singing shells as her play-mates. When she grows up she dreams of marrying Kawelona, the Sunset, so her brother chooses Pupukanioi, Singing Shell, to be his shell carrier for the journey to make his sister's dreams come true. Many kupua join the marriage party as they travel—Kawelona in his cloud boat, Makani-kau in his shell boat and others. These kupua have leaf, flower, plant, bird, shell, cloud, wind, fish, shark, sea moss, stone or cliff bodies. The feast is celebrated at Waipio near the heiau Kahukuwelowelo. Hina takes the body of a lehua, or pohutukawa tree, and after her death, the child who sang and talked to shells, loved and played with them, became the ieie vine which now wreathes the body of the forest goddess."

There are tears in Sahara's eyes. She curls her arm around Cowrie and leans her head on her shoulder.

"Well, you warned me not to get so caught up in pain and anger I couldn't act, Sah. It's important to remind ourselves of why we must fight so hard to protect our natural environment. Finally, it's all we have left. After the age of materialism is over, that's what we'll return to.

Besides, I believe in these stories. I was abandoned as a child, but left with symbols that took me back to my home, my ancestry. I could've ignored them. Mere found me and raised me to treat the ocean and sea shells and trees and birds as friends. She breathed life back into me and sent me out on the ocean to discover the islands I came from."

"And now you breathe life into me." Sahara takes the cowrie shell from her pocket and holds it up to the moon. "I name you Singing Shell, and through you, Cowrie and I will always be connected in soul."

Cowrie smiles. "Ae, Sah. But you'll have to sing waiata to her now."

Sahara grimaces, thinks a moment, then sings a haunting melody telling the tale of a girl who is drowned by her jealous sister and returned as a swan, then is transformed into a harp which sings of the beauty of the countryside. Cowrie is entranced. "Where does that exquisite song come from?" she asks.

"It was written by Loreena McKennitt in Annaghmakerrig. She draws on her Irish ancestry in this song. One sister drowned the other for the sake of a man. They lost their soul sister bond. We must be sure to keep ours, Cowrie."

"Yes, sweet Sah, yes." Cowrie cries, letting out the grief of the past few days of tension, knowing she has found a friend, who, like Peta and Koana, understands her connection to the natural world, the spirit world. A fellow traveller who is willing to work for change, another Heart Warrior.

He toke Koe .... are you a worm?

He toke koe?
Are you a worm?

It is a beautiful calm night. She is floating. Waves lap gently and a feather starfish illuminated by the moon dances, splaying its fairy tentacles, touching her shell as it passes. The starfish skims the surface then dips into the belly of the wave, landing on her back. Mysterious singing sends shivers up her turtle shell, down to her fins. She moves gracefully through the water to the motion of the sounds.

Thwack! "Fou!" Thwack. Voices below. Cowrie wakes with a start. Thwack, more voices, yelling in a foreign language. She swings out of the hammock and rushes to the rail. "Fuck! It's the French! They're trying to board the boat. Piripi! Kuini! Sah—wake them." Sahara pulls on her shorts, grabs her shirt and jumps down the hatch. Mattiu yells something from the wheel. She can't hear. Then a loud-speaker blasts them in French-accented English.

"Theez iz a varning from zee French navy. You must stay out of zee twelve-mile leemeet. Ve have a leeist of conditions. Pleeze let us aboard to deliver zem."

By now Piripi is glaring over the port side. "Kia ora! Please do not board our boat. We will lower a bucket. Put your parcel inside and we will read it. Thank you." He grabs the nearest bucket, still wet with salt water from the last of the crew to vomit inside, and lowers it on the abseiling rope attached to the side of the boat.

110

One of the naval officers, dressed in a wetsuit, tries to stand up in the inflatable to reach the rope and a wave jolts him off balance. His nose goes straight into the sick bucket. Chuckles from the deck. On the next attempt, he grabs the bucket, throws in the rolled-up papers, and tugs it to be raised. "Remember, you have been varned. If you try to enter zee test zone, you vill be in French waters and we vill have to confiscate your boat."

"Yeah, we understand. Thanks." Piripi, always the gentleman, wishes them a safe journey, then turns to the waiting crew. "Ok, everyone. Excitement's over. We'll examine the document in the morning light. Now get your sleep. You may need it." He folds the papers under his arm and descends the ladder backwards.

Cowrie, Kuini and Sahara join Mattiu, Hone and some of the crew at the wheel. As yet, they do not realise that the French navy have delivered a similar message to all boats from the Peace Flotilla who arrive at the nuclear test zone. By Mattiu's reckoning, they are still three kilometres away and with a slight 12-knot night wind, it'd take them a while to get near the danger zone. They decide to have at least two on night watch from now, just in case. Gradually, one by one, they slink back to their beds.

Sahara and Cowrie are wide awake, with no intention of returning to sleep.

"So whad'ya reckon, Sah? Is this intended as scare tactics, or what?"

"If it is, it didn't work. Everyone seems to treat it as a bit of a joke. I can't wait to get my hands on that document to see what it says."

"I'm sure Piripi will reveal all tomorrow. Besides, you've got enough media guff being radioed and faxed to sink a bloody ship, Sah."

111

Sahara grins. "You ain't seen nuttin yet, sistah! Wait till I really get going."

"Trust the bloody French to wake me out of a delicious dream," sighs Cowrie. Sahara begs her to tell. Then she replies with a dream she had at school of making love to the captain of the cricket team on the pitch. All the other kids were watching, egging them on.

"Ugh. Weird. It must have been so strange being the only girl at a boys' school. How did you cope?"

"I loved it actually. I knew I was safe because Uncle Quentin ran the prep school and in some ways it gave me a lot of confidence. I grew up thinking I could do and be anything because boys are raised that way. I always hated that giggly girls' school stuff."

"But didn't you miss that special emotional bonding you can have with women? I mean, most chaps just don't speak about their feelings. But you seem quite good at it."

"I learned that later. It's still hard sometimes. I often hold back. I think I'm a bit of a loner because in many ways I was an outsider at school. I was accepted, but I was still different."

"Maybe that's why we connect so well. I grew up feeling different too—culturally, physically, even emotionally. I threw myself into books and spent a lot of time communing with nature."

"Singing to shells …"

"Yeah … hey, Sah. Have you ever caught up with your mother? You must be curious to know how she is."

"Aunty Daphne always said she'd be looked after, would fall on her feet. Daughter of a princess, she'd say. I never really knew what she meant. After Mother left for France, we didn't hear from her. I think she sent the odd postcard to Uncle Quentin, and money for our education, but no letters to us. If we mentioned her, it upset Dad when we went home on the holidays so I learned not to ask. He did his best for us."

"I can see that. I think he's very proud of you, Sah."

"Yes. We must get some sleep before dawn, Cowrie." Sahara stretches out in her hammock and rolls over.

Cowrie lies awake, wondering how Sahara's mother could possibly abandon such a special daughter. She plays many scenarios in her mind but cannot find one that fits. Eventually, she drifts back to sleep.

Tukua mai he kapunga oneone ki a au hai tangi.
Send me a handful of soil so that I may weep over it.

The next morning they draw up alongside the New Zealand government flagship *Tui* and are invited aboard for breakfast, and to discuss the conditions of their contact. After a powhiri, they settle down to eat. The captain explains that their official role is to protect the Peace Flotilla and provide petrol and supplies when necessary. However, this only applies to those boats encircling the zone and staying their ground as protest vessels. They cannot help any boat which enters the test zone because it is then in French and not international waters. He makes it clear that they have the full support of the New Zealand government, and adds, as an aside, it could be the first time since MMP that all parties have united in opposition to the tests and in support of the protest. That raises a few laughs.

"I can't believe your government would provide so much support for a protest group," Sahara whispers. "Can you see John Major sending government support for the protestors on the Shell rig?" Those nearby chuckle at the thought.

"Finally, welcome aboard. I think Chris Carter, MP, would like to have a word on behalf of the politicians." Everyone cheers.

"He's a great MP and he's openly gay," whispers Cowrie to Sahara, who opens her eyes wide in amazement.

"And spunky too. Pity all the best men are gay."

"Poetic justice, kid. You can join the troops anytime," whispers Cowrie. Sahara blushes and concentrates on her notes.

Chris gives them a moving welcome and reads faxed messages of support from all the political parties in Aotearoa. There is an extraordinary feeling of camaraderie among usually opposing forces—politicians, protesters, Maori activists, the navy, to say nothing of gays on all sides. Sahara has not witnessed such togetherness since her days at Greenham. This unity is a unique angle for her next media release, may help to bring people together in support of the protest back home.

Afterwards, they relax with crew and join a guided tour of the *Tui*. A few naval officers are taken aboard *Manawa Toa* to see the mighty waka. Mattiu and Piripi explain the ancestral significance of the carvings on the canoe. The officers are impressed, but worried about the safety of the waka in the tempestuous seas that can whip up here. After all, they are twelve miles away from the atoll, essentially in open ocean, with no protection. Members of the waka crew assure them that they will not be paddling except on days when the weather forecast is reasonable. Piripi reminds the naval officers that their ancestors sailed and paddled their way across the entire Pacific Ocean and the *Tui* certainly wasn't around to bail them out then. He stresses, however, that they will not be risking lives or the waka for they must return the canoe intact to the iwi. The naval officers appear worried and ask him to make sure they are alerted when the waka is launched. Piripi agrees.

Petty Officer Pilgrim inspects the equipment, compass and navigational computer on board the *Manawa Toa* to make sure they are in good working condition. He expresses surprise that such an ancient trawler could be so well equipped. Mattiu cannot resist a sharp reply. "Hey, mate, you're lookin at Ngati Cyberspace here. We ain't no pakeha-eating cannibals, ya know. Mind you, wouldn't say no to a bite out of that muscular politician fella you got on board your waka!" The petty officer is so shocked he stands rigid at the wheel, then, realising it's a joke, laughs weakly, turning beetroot red. "Hey, you wanna can that cheek colour, man. Wattie's'd pay ya a fortune to beef up their beet juice!" Matt guffaws loudly, enjoying the chance to make fun of a petty officer under fairly safe circumstances. Pilgrim grins, secretly enjoying the attention, but thinking he'll get back at this bugger one day.

Sahara interviews some of the women naval officers to get their perspectives on the importance of naval involvement in such protest action. The *Manawa Toa* crew are reluctant to leave after such a welcome, but by late afternoon they call it a day and let the officers get on with their tasks.

That evening, they sight *Rainbow Warrior II* and make contact by cell phone. They agree to meet the next morning to discuss tactics. Piripi convenes a meeting of their own crew to debate where the *Manawa Toa* stands regarding vital isssues like entering the test zone should Greenpeace ask them to. It is agreed that only the inflatable lifeboat should enter the zone, leaving the *Manawa Toa* and waka safe in international waters.

"But what if the French confiscate our boat because the inflatable gets caught?"

"I'm sure that'd be illegal, Kuini, since the French only have jurisdiction over the waters surrounding Moruroa to the twelve-mile limit. Outside that, we're protected."

116

After lengthy korero, it is decided that the inflatable is their action protest boat and the crew driving it should be willing to be taken into French custody if it gets heavy. That they'll offer this to Greenpeace so long as it is clear that the *Manawa Toa* and waka are safe. Debate ensues as to who should crew the inflatable. Many oppose women being in such a dangerous role—but they cannot argue against the fact that Cowrie and Sahara have by far the most activist experience. Finally, they vote that both should crew alongside the most experienced men—Piripi and Mattiu. Should such an emergency occur, Eruera would captain the boat, Kuini would cook and Irihapeti would continue to control the media releases and maintain contact with the *Tui* and other flotilla craft. Sahara will be given a cell phone to relay messages back to the boat, which Iri will then fax or radio to overseas media.

The hui ended, they disperse to complete the day's tasks. Drinking tea on the deck later, Kuini, Cowrie, Irihapeti, Marie-Louise and Sahara discuss tactics should anything go wrong. Since three of them are key messengers, it is vital their lines of communication are clear.

"Do you really think we'll enter the test zone?" asks Sahara.

"Depends on Greenpeace tomorrow. I can't imagine that they'd come all this way and not enter the exclusion zone," replies Cowrie.

"How risky will it be?"

Marie-Louise tells them that they'd better be prepared for the worst. "I can assure you the military have rehearsed these scenarios. They will capture you at all costs. Their intention will be to try to board the *Rainbow Warrior* as early as possible in order to confiscate the media equipment. The last thing they want the world

117

seeing is violent action against protesters or photos of cracks in the atoll. They'll be praying that Greenpeace, and any other Peace Flotilla members, will cross that line so they can legitimately confiscate boats, equipment and personnel."

"Yeah, but what would they do with us?"

"Probably not harm you. Too many repercussions. They're more interested in making sure the tests take place and that any protest is kept out of the media. They couldn't care less about you as people."

"That's what I'm worried about," admits Cowrie.

They discuss possible scenarios, then part for bed. Sahara relishes the chance to be directly involved in the action.

"Steady on Sah. We haven't talked to Greenpeace yet. Are you scared, deep inside?"

"Yeah."

"Me too."

"You rethinking, Cowrie?"

"No way. This is what I came for. I just didn't think it'd all happen so soon. I mean, we haven't even launched the waka yet."

"I can't wait to see that. I must get good video footage to send out. Do you think we should suggest a trial run in the inflatable tomorrow after the meeting, and I can film the launching of the waka from surface level?"

"Great idea, Sah. Now get ya beauty sleep, girl. We're gonna need all the energy we can muster."

"Ok. I'll make sure we take the Singing Shell with us Cowrie. For protection."

"We might need more than that against the French, if the bombing of the first *Rainbow Warrior* is anything to go by."

"It's worked against their gendarmes already, Cowrie!"

"Yeah, but we're not up against street cops now. We're up against trained defence forces protecting the military presence of France in the Pacific. We can't afford to forget that."

Sahara breathes deeply, letting the air out through her teeth in a whistle. "Did I tell you how a group of us cut through barbed wire fence, crept past armed guards and climbed on top of the silos at Greenham Common? I never thought I'd have the courage. But once we'd cut the fence, the adrenalin rushed in and nothing could've stopped us."

Cowrie grins. "So that was you, eh, Sah? I remember seeing the media pictures and screaming with glee. And, you'll never guess, but I met a fisherman in Hawai'i, Vile, who told us he'd heard from a fisherman in Aotearoa that 'his wife and a bunch of Pommy sheilas had got in and painted the silos with peace symbols'."

"That was us. Oh my God, it must have been Moira Rakete. Her husband was a fisherman and she was always telling us hilarious tales of their exploits. She missed him terribly while at Greenham. Eventually, his relatives raised the airfare for him to join her. I got a postcard from them in Devon. They were working in a pub there. He served and she sang. They wanted to raise enough money to travel to Ireland then back home."

"Moira Rakete. Well, I'll be damned. I knew she'd buggered off somewhere. She went to school at Kaitaia with one of my cuzzies, then left for England as soon as she earned the fare. Never heard about her since."

"Small planet, huh?"

"Getting smaller by the minute, Sah. I wish Vile was alive so I could tell him what happened to his mate. Vile and his mates rebuilt an ancient stone temple, destroyed by the military on a sacred Hawai'ian island they'd taken over. Koho'olawe. They did it in the dead of night, carrying the stones from the water to the peak. On the last night, swimming back to their outrigger, an explosion burst into the sky from the heiau. Some said it was the military blowing it up, others that it was the Volcano Goddess, Pele, showing her fury at the military invasion of their sacred island."

"Wow! What an amazing story. I vaguely remember Moira telling us something about that, but she missed out the Pele bit."

"That's the best part!"

"Yes. But what an inspiration to us, Cowrie! Just the image of courage we need for this protest action."

"Yeah and so intimately linked, eh? US military invasion of Hawai'i, French invasion of Tahiti, both raping Pacific Islands for their own ends under the guise of paternalistic protection. We'll stop the buggers yet."

"And this time we've got most of the world behind us, even if their governments are reluctant to affirm their support."

"You bet! Think about it Sah. We've got a Frog scientist, a Pommy media queen, Maori activists, Maohi and Maori paddlers, dykes, queers, politicians and no doubt an international contingent on the *Rainbow Warrior*. In the Peace Flotilla, there are lawyers, doctors, chefs, teachers, nurses and community workers, among others. This is the new world order in action!"

"Let's hope so. I'm off to Fairyland." Sahara slides into her hammock.

"Promise, Sah?" Cowrie jokes.

"Go to sleep, Turtle."

Cowrie smiles, imagining the celebration when the French announce that they'll stop the tests. Somehow, despite all her energy, she can't quite see it happening that smoothly. Fate may yet prove her right.

Uenuku-kopako kai awe whare.
Uenuku-kopako eats the soil from his own house.

Spray splashes their faces, wetting the equipment. "Further up, Piripi. I want a shot of the waka being lowered from beneath," yells Sahara. Piripi motors closer until the inflatable is alongside *Manawa Toa*.

"That's as close as I can safely go," he shouts.

"Just a bit further," begs Sahara, sitting astride the rubber prow to balance herself.

"Bloody media wahine!" Piripi whispers.

"I heard that, bro," warns Cowrie, grinning.

"Well, you're responsible for her, Cowrie. Just make sure she stays in the boat. She'd do anything for the right shot."

I wish, thinks Cowrie, secretly. She holds Sahara's wetsuit belt to stop her going overboard. Wake from the *Manawa Toa* slaps into them, knocking her into Cowrie. "Steady on, girl. I know you wanna be intimate, but now's not the time," Cowrie whispers. Sahara bounces back into position as the waka, paddlers aboard, is lowered with the equipment usually employed for pulling up nets bursting with fish. Chanting from within the waka echoes over the water. Once afloat, the paddlers strike out to get clear of the boat, followed by the inflatable, Sahara and her video at the prow.

They paddle the waka in a slow semi-circle, turning to face the atoll. Pita Tangaroa rises from the helm to lead the haka issued as a challenge to the military invasion of

121

Moruroa. The crew use their paddles to stomp the foot rhythms which accompany the haka and at the end raise the hoea above their heads spearing the sky in protest. Pita blows farewell through the conch shell and the paddlers strike out for their first lap around the exclusion zone. The air is electric as cheers from *Manawa Toa*, *Rainbow Warrior* and *Tui* blast out in support of the waka.

Aboard the Greenpeace boat, media rush to the bow to get footage of the mighty canoe, knowing this will be aired all over the world for its visual impact, even on conservative stations which are reluctant to cover protest action. The All Blacks have cemented the haka, in its crudest performance, as a recognisable challenge. Even redneck sports fans will prick up their ears when this is televised. *Manawa Toa* follows the waka at a safe distance, keeping an eye on the rapidly changing weather conditions.

The inflatable remains behind to practise manoeuvres with Greenpeace zodiacs. At this morning's meeting, they accepted the *Manawa Toa* offer to join forces to enter the exclusion zone should the French go ahead with the tests. The aim is to create enough media coverage and attention to have the tests called off, but none are so naive as to believe the French will bow to even the strongest pressure. Should they enter the test zone, the idea is for Piripi's boat to act as a distraction for the French to follow, while the Greenpeace inflatables make an effort to reach the atoll and hide. The Rubber Crews, as they are known, must keep plans entirely secret.

After practice manoeuvres, involving getting crew from one boat to another in an emergency, pulling crew from the water, chasing and being chased by imaginary Frenchmen, they board the *Rainbow Warrior* for further discussions. This time, Cowrie and Sahara get a chance to explore the boat. Stephanie Mills, the Pacific co-ordinator from Aotearoa, shows them the impressive media room. They intend locking themselves in if they are forcibly boarded, in order to keep sending out information. They've reinforced the room especially.

While one of the crew explains how the equipment works, Cowrie remembers the shock and sadness she felt when she first saw pictures of the pioneer *Rainbow Warrior* listing on her side in Auckland harbour, half sunk after the French government agents attached a bomb to her underside and blew a hole in her hull. Visions of Fernando Pereira's body floating to the surface have haunted her for years. Blasted apart in the explosion as he tried to grab his camera gear before they abandoned ship. Trapped in an underwater grave for his bravery.

"A penny for them, Cowrie," Sahara whispers, when the technician has finished.

"Just recalling the first *Warrior*, Sah. They blasted her apart because she was involved in helping Rongelap Islanders protest nuclear testing. What might they do to this boat, to us?"

"We'll just have to wait and see. This time it'll be before the eyes of millions. They wouldn't dare."

"Don't underestimate them, Sah. Auckland harbour is not exactly private. Mind you, they had no idea our investigators and public would be so sharp, that we'd eventually nab their top agents."

"Well, maybe that will warn them against violence this time."

"Hope so. Anyway, I couldn't think of anyone I'd rather go down with, Sah."

"You're not being suggestive again, Cowrie, are you?"

Sahara confronts her, grinning. They both laugh as Cowrie realises what she means.

"Not this time. Ya got me on that one!"

They have dinner with the *Warrior* crew, sharing stories of their protest actions, songs from their countries, late into the night. The *Manawa Toa* and waka crew are not due back until the next day. Cowrie tries to teach them waiata and they urge Piripi and Mattiu to perform a haka. Traditionally, wahine do not take part in haka, but Piripi motions Cowrie to join them. They explain this one is a powhiri or welcome chant, but can be a haka if issued in challenge. On the third round, the crew join in, their voices echoing through the *Rainbow Warrior* and out over the still water, the waves carrying their challenge toward the atoll. The *Rainbow* crew yells out the refrain "te waka ... te waka".

On board *Manawa Toa*, they can hear the paddlers urging themselves on by chanting. Below deck, Irihapeti smiles as the familiar "te waka" greets her ears.

From the canoe, Pita feels a distant vibration. He asks the paddlers to be silent. They peer into the night air. In the far distance, an eerie rumbling. By now, the *Manawa Toa* crew are at the rails, wondering what stopped the paddlers.

Aboard *Rainbow Warrior*, the haka gains momentum. Through it, someone is yelling. A voice blasts out of the radio room. "The bastards!" A second of silence while the operator turns up the volume.

The silent waka glides over the water. There is static on the intercom. Irihapeti turns it full volume to decipher the voice. It booms out over the water: "I repeat. This is the HMS *Tui*. We have detected an underground nuclear explosion on screen. We are seeking verification from the

124

New Zealand Geological Centre. This is an alert to all members of the Peace Flotilla. Please stay calm and radio in your positions. It is vital that we can account for everyone. *Manawa Toa*, please advise if your waka is safe," then more static. Irihapeti chokes back tears of anger. "*Manawa Toa* calling HMS *Tui*. Both boat and waka crew safe. I repeat. We are safe and positioned 12.5 miles from Moruroa Atoll, south-east of Tui." "Thank you. Calling *Rainbow Warrior*, can you verify position of smaller craft ..." The voices echo out over the water, piercing the night air, reminding them how vulnerable they are, how vital their contact is.

Later, surging waves created by the explosion send wash over the waka, blasting into the side of *Manawa Toa*. The paddlers struggle to maintain balance. Anxiety grips the crew. Then calm, as the waves subside. Suddenly, Pita rises and leads them into the most powerful haka Irihapeti has ever heard. It resounds over the water, is heard on the intercom by all the flotilla tuned in. Cheers of angry support and defiance surge through the microphones, out over the black waves, into every piece of floating seaweed, shell, whale and dolphin still alive after the nuclear underwater explosion. Their survival depends on the force of this haka.

As Pita blows into the conch to sound their defiance an orca whale responds, launching her huge body over the prow of the waka, sounding a haunting cry. The paddlers salute her with paddles raised to the heavens like spears. She responds with another mighty call, flinging herself back over the prow, then dives into the black depths. Pita smiles. It is a sign. Their haka has been heard.

Ehara taku toa i te toa takitahi engari te toa takitini.
My strength is not that of the individual but that of the multitudes.

The Maohi crew members who joined *Manawa Toa* at Pape'ete share their whakapapa with the Nga Puhi, Tainui and Te Arawa iwi on board and talkstory well into the night. One of the crew mixes up some kava and this is appreciated all round.

"To all of us who have survived and those who died for the cause." Piripi raises his coconut cup and bows his head in respect. The sounds of hollowed-out coconuts clinking in the night air are haunting, as if the skeletons of their relatives are returning to collaborate in the struggle, to sing through their bones that their deaths have not been in vain.

Roimata weeps convulsively, then between gasps, tells of her whanau. "My chile—first born—she die of cancer. Second one has leukemia. Third—he die at two months. Nobody know why. Fourth—she born early—has anudder condition. Fifth—he get so sick we have to bury him and I cry for three weeks until fadder come to collek me and I in white man's hospital for weeks and weeks. I start to lose memories. I never forget that place tho. One night—all my chilluns come to see me in my dreams. They ask me, one by one, to make it right for next chilluns. That why I am here now. For them, not for me. For all the udders who lost their chilluns to diseases brought by the French bombs. They say we have work and hospitals now—but what use is they when we no

126

have our chilluns?" Kuini slips her strong arm around Roimata's back, supporting her, as she weeps and weeps.

How can a mother live when her five children have died? How can anybody pretend this is natural, this is coincidence, when so many similar tales are told? Sahara listens in the background, stunned to hear Roimata's tale, and shocked that the French have so skilfully kept the stories contained within the islands.

"How does the world not know these cases?" she ventures to ask.

Rangi replies. "Heaps of Maohi have cancer or leukemia or some related illness. They usually get sent to Paris and nobody knows what happens to them. But us Maohi—we do not parade our young ones about with their sores and illnesses. It is not our way to do that. So when the scientists and doctors come to ask where these kids are, most families join ranks and hide them. That suits the French fine. They do not want these stories getting out. They still say there are no victims of the tests, that the high death rate is cos we do not know how to take care of our children and we do not use the hospitals enough. Funny thing is, before the French came, we had a much lower death rate and none of these deformed babies with two heads and three legs and four arms. That only began after the testing. But they still deny it. They say it is our lifestyle. Ha. What lifestyle? Nuked fish and now we have to eat canned tuna to be sure it is nuke-free. Fish are our lifeblood. We are islands surrounded by sea—and here we are reduced to eating canned fish. *Vraiment*—it's disgusting!" Rangi speaks his adopted language with gruff tones, throwing the words out into the ocean as if spitting them away.

Marie-Louise confirms the reports of "*bébé martyre d'atomique*" and says she was asked by the French government to destroy all anecdotal reports and documentation of abnormal deaths after atomic and nuclear testing began. She adds that some of the "genetic abnormalities", babies born with hideous cancerous growths, were flown secretly by the military to France for further tests to be done. That none of them survived because they were used as experiments to see what drugs might be useful if the nuclear tests ever affected the French military personnel or civilians.

"So what is to separate the Nazis doing such experimentation on Holocaust victims secretly and the French doing it today—when we all believe such atrocities could never happen again? Are we going to be the witnesses who say we never knew it was happening therefore we are saved from blame?" spits out Kuini in anger.

"My ancestors have Jewish as well as Maohi blood. My grandmother is a survivor of the Holocaust and she escaped on a cargo boat to these islands, only to be faced with a modern holocaust and the loss of three of her mokopuna to leukemia at the hands of the French. She says only the academics and scientists and governments will make the distinctions in naming. For those of us who are victims—one holocaust is as bad as another. We do not get to choose which degree of suffering we endure. We simply pull together to survive. Our only hope is in mass protest and mass education. And we need all the help we can get in this. That is why I am glad Marie-Louise has jumped ship and joined our side after losing Rua, and that Sahara is here to help record this and get it to a European audience. We must work together for our mutual survival—or we are doomed to suffer endless variations of the Holocaust. All indigenous people have endured some form of extinction by induced diseases, bombs or false treaties. Let the academics debate the terminology. I'm here to fight for my people." Rangi raises his cup of kava and throws it out to the heavens, adding, "Bear witness to our struggle. We will not be silenced or forgotten."

He holds his empty coconut shell to his stomach and lets out a blood-curdling wail, as if enacting a tangi for all victims. The sky answers with a resounding, hollow silence. Then, from portside, an orca leaps from the water, her entire body flying through the midnight air, and they watch until her flukes disappear into the black ocean depths. The crew hold their collective breath in awe. Then Kuini leads them into a waiata telling the tale of Pakake, which Piripi follows with a haka, until the boat shakes with their stamping feet and the skies resound with slapping thighs, as if a collective drumbeat of resistance has spiked the quiet heavens, broken through the colonial silencing.

Nga kanohi o te rangi.
Stars, the eyes of the sky.

The next day, an urgent meeting is held for those from the Peace Flotilla willing to enter the test zone with Greenpeace. They want several inflatables to distract the French while their own craft zoom to the atoll. Action is scheduled for the first night of the new moon, when an eclipse will appear making it difficult for the military to keep track of small vessels in the dark. Everyone is briefed on the danger and some groups drop out because they cannot reach consensus on putting their crew at such risk. All the crews still involved are sworn to secrecy.

Back on *Manawa Toa*, Irihapeti yells for Cowrie. "Quick, it's Koana and Mauva on the phone." Koana apologises for not making it to Pape'ete in time for their visit and updates them on progress since. There have been more street riots. Mauva thanks them for rescuing Raoul and says he healing well. They are keen to know how the explosion felt at sea. Koana says that Sahara's pictures of the riot appeared in local and international papers and caused outrage from supporting groups. Cowrie is bursting to tell them about the planned action but cannot. But when Mauva asks how far they are willing to go, she replies "as far as we possibly can". She figures they'll work it out from the hint.

Later, they call Te Kotuku Marae and Mere senses Cowrie may be getting involved too deeply. "You just be

130

careful, Turtle. I know you'll be itching to get into the action. Just remember the sunken *Rainbow*. Be vigilant." Cowrie promises to take care. Faxes and messages from Aotearoa and the Pacific have reached the marae, and the crew of *Manawa Toa* are encouraged by their support. Mere tells them that there have been street marches in Aotearoa and a ban on buying French products. French bakeries have had to close down and wine sales are dropping. A television station polled 93 per cent of New Zealanders behind the protest action. Hone grabs the microphone to say that the other 7 per cent are Frogs or Poms! That raises a chuckle, but Mere warns them not to play the nationality game, that they must remember it's government military action they are protesting.

Throughout the day, they listen to media reports from around the world. There is protest and outrage in Germany, the Netherlands, Belgium, France and England. But the French and English governments support the necessity for tests. Sahara is outraged. The USA denounces the resumption of testing. It looks as if France will be isolated, but for English support.

The next few nights, the inflatables rehearse their plans on water. The French navy keep an eye on them from a distance. They know something is up.

Their first mail delivery is airlifted onto the *Tui* and distributed as crew arrive for fresh water supplies. Cowrie and Sahara lie in their hammocks avidly reading their correspondence. It strengthens their resolve.

Cowrie learns that Peta and Nanduye are working in New York. The US government is suggesting a kind of bulk funding for all people of colour. They want to cut federal treaty links with Indians and throw a bundle of money at local governments. Each group will have to fight for resources, which pitches Blacks, Jews, Poles,

Indians and other nationalities against each other. Peta stresses the importance of their action against colonial nuclear powers in the Pacific. "Indigenous people around the globe have their eyes focused on the Pacific. It's a symbol for all our struggles. Do all you can, Turtle. We're with you in spirit."

"Cowrie, can I use some of this information for my next article? So few of the newspaper reports have stressed the colonial connection. They're all busy focusing on nuclear weapons alone. They are not even asking how these weapons ever came into the Pacific, or whether the French have a right to be here."

"Please do, Sahara. It'll get more press coming from you with your UK connections. Here's Peta's letter." Cowrie hands it over. Sahara takes notes and asks questions from time to time. Later, she reads Cowrie part of a letter from her brother Crispin who is working as a naturalist in Antarctica. He describes minke whales feeding at the foot of Endurance Glacier, how they glide hauntingly through the deep blue waters then dive deep to feast on krill. Next to him, a whale has suddenly surfaced through a crack in the ice separating a group of Weddell seals basking on the surface. They slip into the flowing water and disappear from sight. He tells how he spent last December watching young albatross chicks on Bird Island. One of their parents had been caught in a fishing net and its neck was rubbed raw from the plastic string. They managed to rescue her, but many others had been killed this way. He describes the awesome sight of icebergs towering above them in the mist as they float past documenting the currents.

"Imagine living in the Antarctic. I could do with some of that ice on my body right now. How long has he been there, Sah?"

"Two years so far. He goes down for the summer season. The meteorologists and a few others stay all winter, but there's little light and they're mostly underground."

"So what does he do for the rest of the year?"

"He works in Edinburgh as a naturalist, but he's also a dancer. Usually does a show for the festival."

"Really? An Ice Dancer, eh?"

Sahara laughs. "No, but he'd like that description. In fact, I think you'd get on well. He's a loner and a bit of a dreamer too."

"Look who's talking, Sah!" Cowrie laughs. "Send him aroha from us if you write back. Tell him we'll be down to visit next summer—if we survive the test zone, that is!"

"Would you really want to go? I've been dreaming of joining him as a research assistant for months now. I want to write about the ecology issues and the problem of recycling waste down there."

"As well as the wildlife and nature, I'd hope?"

"Yes, both. Dream on, eh, Cowrie?"

"Well, your bro made it, Sah. So you could too. But we've got work to do here first. Got that article finished yet? I'll check it if ya like."

"Thanks. Here it is." Sahara hands over her first draft. "Cowrie, you know the orca that Pita described, which crossed the prow of the waka just after the first nuclear explosion?"

"Yeh?"

"Do you think it was a sign in some way? You know, like Opo was for the Hokianga?"

"I'm sure of it, Sah. As real as your singing cowrie shell. You have to believe in the connectedness of nature as our ancestors did."

"Including my Irish ancestors?"

"Absolutely. It was in that song you sang me."

Sahara hums the song as an orange glow lights up the azure horizon. Deep beneath them, black and white orca are swimming, trying to readjust their sonar after the underwater explosion several days ago. They have been veered off their usual course. They struggle to get their bearings, may end up stranded on a beach in Tahiti or Aotearoa while humans speculate on why they appear to have these strange suicidal pacts.

Kua mate te marama.
The moon is dead.

Piripi checks the provisions stored on the inflatable while Mattiu inspects the engine and fuel supply. It's 11 pm and they are due to meet the other crews at midnight. Marie-Louise has predicted the eclipse of the moon will take place at approximately 1.30 am and last for twenty minutes. That gives them time to cross over into French waters in the dark. Once the sickle moon reappears, the *Manawa Toa* zodiac will lead a chase for the French navy inflatables to follow, allowing the Greenpeace zodiacs to flee for the atoll. With luck, they will not be seen or captured.

Mattiu has attached a silencer to the engine, which they will take off to attract attention to the zodiac once the others have begun their flight over water. They set out in silence. As if the night before a storm, there is an eerie quietness and calm. Clad in black wetsuits inside a charcoal rubber boat, their silhouettes are barely visible as they skim across the surface of the glassy ocean. As arranged, Cowrie utters the call of a takapu to attract the other zodiacs toward them. Silence. She tries again. Way in the distance, a gannet echoes. Is it them or a real bird? They wait, drifting. Finally, a zodiac slips in behind. Then another. They lie waiting on the edge of the test zone. On the far horizon they can see the lights of the French navy ship guarding the waters. The *Manawa Toa* crew must keep it in their sights.

1.30 arrives. Still a faint glow of moon over water. Enough to be seen. 1.33, 1.35 … 1.40. They consider whether it's worth the risk to radio back to Marie-Louise to check. Suddenly, the eclipse brings total darkness. Idling zodiacs sweep into action and surge out towards the atoll in unison, like a wave rolling toward the waiting shore in perfect motion. The crews are spread flat over the rubber surface with their helmsmen facing the dark. Only the whites of their eyes are visible as they fly over the water, dark riders on black stallions streaking through the night. Adrenalin, fear and commitment tug at their guts. Sheer speed makes them hang onto their furious beasts pounding the turbulent waters they create around themselves. They must cover as much ocean as possible with the taonga of darkness nature has granted them.

Cowrie glances at Sahara. She is a sleek seal skimming through sea, her skin tightly woven around her, fins tucked underneath, flippers trailing out the back. A selkie, touched by the call of the wild. The black water is deep with danger. At any moment they could hit a whale or driftwood, a partly submerged container from an abandoned ship. She stares at the lights of the French navy vessel. It doesn't appear to have moved. Night folds around them with a seemingly endless darkness. Like flying into death, into infinity on the wings of a bird barely skimming the surface of the water, sure of its flight but uncertain of the risks ahead. This must be what it's like in the Antarctic wilderness in mid-winter. She recalls flashes of Crispin's letter, sliding down a frozen river in obscurity, not knowing what lies ahead … endless nights listening to the sound of the pack ice forming, the waves being captured and frozen in mid-flight under a cloak of darkness.

A sickle moon emerges from her blanket, the signal to part ways. The others skim toward the atoll while they veer to starboard where they will cross the path of the French navy searchlights. It is dim, with only a few feet of water ahead of them visible. Still risky.

They must appear as if heading toward the atoll to distract the navy. Nothing yet. They cut the motor and drift a while in the semi-dark. The naval vessel has remained static. Almost too good to be true. The crew grin at each other, pleased they have achieved the first stage of their mission.

Then suddenly, out of the sky, a huge whirring bird. Searchlights skim the water and capture the zodiac in full beam. Mattiu crunches her into gear and the chase is on. "Shit! I didn't realise they had copters on board. This'll make it easy for them to spot the other crews."

"Not if we divert their attention. Hit it, Matt," yells Piripi. "Heads down you two."

They speed in the direction of *Manawa Toa*, hoping they'll make it before the inflatables from the navy vessel intercept. Cowrie glances up. The chopper is whirring dangerously close, almost on top of them, whipping up the water and slowing their pace. Out of its belly, a huge oval egg emerges with a tail dangling down. They drop it into the ocean. It's a zodiac with frogmen strapped aboard, the tail its motor. It whirrs into action, as Matt spins them in the opposite direction. Sahara bounces over the side, one arm and leg grasping the zodiac. Cowrie hauls her back in, clipping her belt onto the ropes. Shots fire over their heads.

"Christ. Didn't think they'd shoot at us."

"Stay down you two. They're only trying to scare us. They're shooting above our heads. Just hold on and pray," Piripi yells, struggling to be heard above the whirring copter and the roar of the engine. By now the French zodiac is parallel. The copter swoops low in a threatening gesture and more shots are fired. Through a megaphone, a voice warns them that they are in French waters and must stop or face the consequences.

Fury takes over fear in Sahara as she lies on the bottom of the craft and aims her video up at the copter. She captures it swooping down again and more shots firing, then focuses her lens on the zodiac ramming them. By now the adrenalin is racing through their bodies. The zodiac rams again, and a frogman tries to board their inflatable. Matt spins around and loses him in the water. The frogmen have to turn to pick up their man. The *Manawa Toa* zodiac spins past the Frenchmen, spraying them with water. Sahara laughs, capturing it on film. The copter swoops down and lowers a second inflatable. Matt drenches it with waves as they skim close and whisk away a few seconds before impact.

The cat-and-mouse games continue for about twenty minutes, then the copter zooms down and flings out a huge net, capturing both boats in its grip. All hell breaks loose. The net clogs the motors and there is yelling and cursing. From the whirring monster in the sky, they must look like ants trying to crawl out of a saucer of poison.

Cowrie slips her fish knife from the sheath strapped to her ankles and begins cutting herself out of the mesh. The others follow her actions. Sahara pokes her lens through the large holes in the net and keeps filming. After cutting herself free, Cowrie begins slashing the net over Sahara. "Stop filming, Sah! I don't want my mug all over news screens wielding a knife at close range. Not a good image for peaceful protest!" She lashes at the net around Sahara's arms, then works her way down to her legs. By now Piripi and Matt are free, but the boat is still caught in the web. They begin cutting it from the craft, being careful not to puncture the rubber.

Nearby, the frogmen struggle to cut themselves free. Their zodiac is twice as large, with twice as many crew. Matt cannot start the motor, so dives over the back to slice the ropes. They French are yelling and cursing. Suddenly the copter swoops low and gives orders in French. The second zodiac, which had come to the rescue of the first, leaves them and scoots out toward the atoll. "Looks like they've found out we're not alone," whispers Cowrie. Matt flings himself back into the craft and tells them to belt themselves in. He pulls the motor. It is dead. Again and again. Water pours from his face. Suddenly, it zooms into life. He throttles back and yells at Cowrie and Sahara to hold the rest of the netting above them as they pick their way clear.

By now the frogmen have nearly cut themselves free. They use the netting to pull closer to the *Manawa Toa* crew. Cowrie sees them edging alongside, about five metres away, then three, then one. Another few seconds and the French will be on board. Cowrie flicks her knife from its sheath, kisses it farewell, and aims directly for the rubber hull at the front of the French zodiac to avoid hurting anyone. The knife soars through the air and hits the target perfectly. A hissing is heard and the front compartment of the French zodiac deflates, lowering the stunned frogmen into the water, while their companions rush aft. There is chaos and cursing. Piripi grins. "Perfect shot. Kia ora, Cowrie." A few more minutes of manoeuvring through the water and they are clear. Matt crunches the zodiac into gear and they shoot into the night, heading toward *Manawa Toa*, hotly pursued by the second copter.

We cannot see how to thread worms in the dark...

E kore e kitea te tui i nga toke i te pouri.
We cannot see how to thread worms in the dark.

Kuini and Marie-Louise hang over the rail of *Manawa Toa*, peering into the distance.

"Can't see a bloody thing. It's misty out there. Especially after the eclipse. I hope they're ok."

"They'll be safe, Queenie," she assures. "The French wouldn't dare harm them with all this media attention around."

"Yeah, but where's the media now? I mean, who knows what they're doing?"

"*Vrai*. All we can do is trust the crews will be safe."

"After the *Rainbow Warrior* bombing, I doubt that Aotearoans will ever trust them again. It was the last straw. You know, like that moment when a wife finally sees the light and leaves the fella who's been bashing her up for years?"

"*Oui*, but you trusted me enough to let me aboard."

"You're different. You've worked in protest against French nuking of our islands."

"Most of my family and friends back in France also support the end of testing. It's more complex than ..." Marie-Louise freezes mid-sentence as shots ring out in the distance. She looks at Kuini nervously. "*Mon Dieu!* I hope I do not have to eat my words." She peers into the water, as if it might hold the secret to her silent question.

Kuini rushes down to the radio room. "Iri, notify the *Tui* and *Rainbow Warrior* that we've heard shots. Try to find out what's happened."

Irihapeti hesitates a moment. "Does that mean I have to tell the *Tui* our boats are out there?"

"If necessary, yes. Play it by ear."

Irihapeti cannot reach the *Rainbow Warrior* because the lines are busy. But *Tui* comes in clearly. She reports gunshots, asks if they have heard them. *Tui* replies that they have, but they seem to be in the far distance, well away from the flotilla. Iri takes a deep breath.

"Inflatables from the *Rainbow Warrior* and *Manawa Toa* are heading for the atoll. Greenpeace hopes to make it to Moruroa and our crew are attempting to divert the French."

"Shit, now you've put us in one helluva position. Officially we are supposed to cut all contact if any of the flotilla enter the test zone. But we'll see what we can find out. Notify us if they return. I'll call if we get news. Over and out."

The silence is sudden. They could find themselves completely isolated. It dawns on them they are alone out here. Once you've gone over the line, it's too late to go back.

"Let me know if you hear anything. I'm shooting up to the deck." Kuini grabs a cell phone and climbs the narrow stairs into the night air. She tries to make contact with the cell phone attached to Sahara's waist. Nothing. Not even static. Could be out of range.

The next twenty minutes are agonising. They can hear a copter whirring but cannot locate it. The French navy is too far away to see if there's any action aboard. Suddenly a buzz on the cell phone. Kuini nearly jumps out of her skin. She grabs the receiver and yells.

"Sahara?"

"No, it's Iri. Just reporting that the *Rainbow Warrior* have radioed through. They think at least one of their boats has reached the atoll, and French zodiacs are pursuing the other boats."

"Any mention of specific crew?"

"Na. That's it, Kuini. Hang in there. I'll keep you posted."

"Kia ora."

Kuini tries calling Sahara again. This time there is static, yelling, shots. The French are close enough to be heard. The phone is switched on, but Sahara is not answering. Maybe she's left it going so they can hear the action? Maybe she's hurt? Maybe the others are dead? Maybe they're in the French boat? No, then the phone would have been taken. A hundred scenarios flash through her head. Other crew on *Manawa Toa* gather round, all thinking the worst once they hear the shots and French voices yelling. No sound from the captives at all. Then the cell phone cuts dead. Utter silence but for the waves lapping their prow.

"Can we risk taking the waka to check on them?" asks Kuini.

"We shouldn't. We promised we'd bring her home safely," Eruera replies, "but this is different. There's no back-up for our crew out there. I say we vote on it. Who's willing to come?" One by one, all the paddlers raise their hands. But there's one place spare, the Tainui fella who came down with food poisoning last night. Eruera turns around. "We need a Tainui paddler to replace Wiremu. You up to it, Kuini?"

Kuini looks at the men, gauging whether they'll protest. They remain silent. "I'd be honoured," she replies, and the crew immediately swings into action. Once the waka is lowered to the water, they test the cell phone Kuini carries. It's relaying back to the boat. But no sound from the zodiac. Eruera leads the haka that will fill them with fighting spirit, protect them while they lash out into the darkness in search of their mates. As they disappear into the night, the ancient "ka mate, ka mate" chant echoes eerily in the wind.

Ehara i te aitanga a Tiki!
Well done, descendant of Tiki!

Kuini suggests they follow the sound of the copter since that's most likely to be where the action is. They strike out chanting haka in their heads, not wanting to attract attention once they cross into the test zone. A light squall chops up the sea around them and they concentrate on their mission, well aware that it's risky in a racing waka not intended for the open oceans. The sky is still dark but they only have a couple of hours to find their crew before dawn breaks. Images of them shot, floating around in the dark, or in French custody crowd Kuini's mind. She's not sure which would be worse. Her arm muscles are bursting. It's some time since she's paddled this hard.

The copter motor whirrs closer. A light beams down, picking out flotsam on the water. Then it is gone again. They are joined by dolphins diving through the water splashing their prow. Silent companions for the journey. Kuini smiles to herself, casting aside all the dangerous scenarios. She focuses on the movement of the dolphins as they dance through the spray. Her arms rise as their bodies rise, fall as they fall. The paddlers are in unison with each other, with the dolphins. Suddenly the mammals alter direction, heading portside. Kuini touches Pita's shoulder, motions toward them. He notices and gives directions to change tack, follow the dolphins. They are now moving away from the copter noise. Within minutes, a cry from the water, as one of the

145

dolphins changes direction and the others follow, the waka with them.

By now Kuini is beginning to worry that these mammals, so playful, are engaging them in a game of fun. Then, a noise to starboard, like paddles. They slow down, wondering if it's the French ready to trap them. It stops. The dolphins nose at the bow, urging them to continue. It can't be the zodiac. No engine noise. So what is it? Maybe an orca spouting? They approach tentatively, making out what appears to be the large black shape of a floating whale, as if sleeping on the surface. As it nears, a voice whispers "kia ora". Kuini shines her torch in the direction of the voice, picking out a small zodiac with four weary paddlers aboard, its motor cut and netting stuck to the sides. Relieved, they glide alongside.

"Kia ora, sis. Give us a lift, eh?" whispers Cowrie, grinning.

"You look buggered. You ok?"

"Yeah, but our motor cut out about an hour ago. These things are wicked to row, mate!" The waka paddlers chuckle and help the crew aboard. Once settled between the feet of paddlers, Kuini radios back to *Manawa Toa*. Iri tells them they are not safe yet. That the *Rainbow Warrior* has radioed. The French have boarded her and are threatening to confiscate the boat as well as any zodiacs caught. It's illegal, but the French play by their own rules.

Kuini communicates this to the waka crew. Piripi takes command. "We'll have to destroy the zodiac and pray we all make it back to *Manawa Toa* before they catch us. Cowrie, let's go swimming." He hands her his spare knife. They zip up their wetsuits and dive into the water, swimming to the zodiac tied at the rear. Blades glint in the moonlight as they slash at the sides, tearing giant rips into her belly. The air is tense. They spent weeks fund-raising for it. But their action may save them from capture. They must do it.

Pita breaks the tense silence. "Ever thought of applying to be French agents?" he whispers as they rip holes in the sides of the boat. He mocks a French accent: "Alain et Dominique battle zee waves for supremacy, making zee 'oles that will decide zee destiny of zeir countwee, zeir fweedom, zeir fyuture. *Liberté, égalité, fraternité!*" The paddlers chuckle at the bizarre commentary in the midst of such danger. The humour breathes new life into them, urges them on. Cowrie dives under the boat, poking her knife up through its belly, then surfaces at the bow. Finally, the zodiac begins to sink, weighed down by the motor. Piripi and Cowrie are hauled into the waka, and the crew strike out for *Manawa Toa*.

Half an hour after they are safely aboard, a copter swoops from the sky and lowers a zodiac to the sea. A French navy contingent approaches the boat and warns them that it is suspected that they have a zodiac in French waters, and if so, all their boats will be confiscated. Marie-Louise replies to them in French, assures them that no zodiac is aboard and all crew are accounted for. An officer boards the boat and asks where their zodiac is.

"Down there, in the water," Piripi answers, emerging dry onto the deck, pointing over the rail.

"But where? I don't see it," replies the officer.

"The canoe, monsieur. The waka. That's our zodiac."

The officer looks at him in disbelief. "But where is zee motor?"

"No motor, mate," replies Mattiu. "Just these." He ripples his arm muscles in the face of the officer who blanches and steps back.

"You are mad. *Foux*. Ve vill find zee zodiac, never fear." After a thorough search of the boat, no trace of the inflatable is found. The officer repeats they will find "zee zodiac", then disappears down the rope ladder to his waiting boat.

"Poor bugger," Piripi announces to those around. "I think he was the one whose face ended up in our sick bucket. I guess he won't forget us in a hurry." Laughter all around as the crew slip down to the galley for a round of celebration with feijoa champagne they'd saved for such an occasion. "A toast to all the crew!" Sahara slips her video tape into the VCR so they can enjoy the action shots. News comes in that some of the *Rainbow* crew have made it to the atoll and buried themselves in the sand. Another round of feijoa bubbly. They party until dawn, then slink off to their beds for the best sleep in weeks.

Ko Maui tinihanga koe.
Like Maui, you are a deceiver.

It is noon before they wake. The sun is directly behind the mast halyards, casting a shadow like a net over Sahara's face.

"Heh, Sah, you awake?"

"Only just." Sahara opens her eyes, then shuts them instantly. "What time is it, Turtle?"

"After noon. We missed brekkie, but buggered if I'll miss lunch."

"Watch out or you'll end up cooking it." Sahara raises herself on one arm and rubs her eyes.

"You ok, Sah? You look beat."

"I'm all right. Just tired. Had a few nightmares. Being pursued by French-speaking toads. Can't believe we actually survived yesterday."

"Me too. When that bloody net came down on us I didn't think we had a show of getting out. If it wasn't for the Frogs botching up and netting their own crew too, we'd never have made it."

"To say nothing of the canoe rescuing us. How far do you think we'd've got paddling?"

"To be honest, I think we were beginning to go round in circles, but don't tell anyone else I admitted that."

Sahara yawns.

"Hey, you scooped, Sah. Some great video shots."

"I don't know how much we can use. I mean how do we explain them if we weren't out on the water? It's

149

obvious we entered the test zone and it's obvious we were in an inflatable."

"Yeah, but how can they prove it's us? We were all in black wetsuits in a black zodiac. Anyway, can't you just send it out to the media incognito? The French'll probably assume it's Greenpeace and they've already nabbed their boats."

"Too late now," offers Marie-Louise. "The tape went out by courier this morning."

Sahara sits up in surprise "And you let it go, knowing it could put us all in danger?"

"Knew you'd take it that way. We don't have equipment to edit on board so it was a case of meeting the deadline or not. We're here to protest and get our protest known. Your work in this has been invaluable, Sahara. *Merci beaucoup*." She walks away.

"I don't appreciate her doing that," admits Sahara.

"Nor me, but Iri knows where to send them and I'm sure they had to make a decision while we slept."

"They could have woken me."

"Let go of it, Sah. We can't do anything now. Hey, I hope they don't edit out that shot of you under the net when I grabbed the camera through the hole. You looked like a fish gasping for breath, a stunned mullet."

"Felt like it too, Cowrie. Shit, I was scared then. But we made it, huh?"

"Sure did. Hope you had that cowrie shell with you."

"All the time. She was singing through my skin, especially when you were cutting me out of that net. I really thought the French had us when it came down. Took me by surprise."

"Me too. The French tried a Maui trick but it didn't work for them."

"What do you mean?"

"In Hawai'i, the sun is moving so fast Hina has a hard time drying her strips of bark cloth. You know, like that tapa cloth on my wall at home?"

"The brown and cream designs on beaten bark?"

"Yeah. Well, Maui decides to check out where the sun rises at Wailohi. He makes a strong cord from coconut fibre, throws it over the sun to draw her back, and slows her rising."

"Does it work?"

"Sure thing. That's why we have plenty of daylight now. There's a similar story in Aotearoa."

"But the French slowed us down, even if they didn't catch us."

"Ah, yes, but not for good. We escaped. The net's no good if you can cut holes in it, eh?"

Sahara throws her head back and laughs gloriously. "You are incorrigible, Cowrie. You've an answer for everything."

"It's in the blood, sis. You ready for brunch?"

"Yes. I'd like a fresh salad with at least five different lettuce leaves, olives and fetta cheese."

"Fresh lettuce is one delight we can't do out here, Sah. But I could whip you up a Spanish omelette."

"That'll be fine."

Arm in arm, they walk the deck then go single file down the ladder to the galley. Behind them, Marie-Louise is taking notes. Cowrie glances back, wondering if she's as solid as they'd thought. Strange her sending out that tape without checking it with Sahara first.

Ki te hamama popoia te tangata, e kore e mau te ika.
If a man spends his nights yawning, he will not catch any fish.

She is surfing down giant sand dunes, salt air in her face, gritty sand scouring her shoulders, plunging head first towards gigantic waves. She tries to turn back, fall off, roll away but she is glued to the sand board. The first wave towers above her, crashing over her back. She is plunged deep into the belly of the wave. It throws her up into its surf like a whale playing with a seal pup before the kill. Then a crooning sound through the thunderous surf. Her mother's voice, singing to her.

Sahara wakes, startled. Nothing but black sky and bright stars. She makes out the Southern Cross and traces its tail, then follows the wide sweep of the Milky Way, trying to calm herself after the nightmare. The vulnerability of being tossed about in the sea stays with her, frightens her. Why has her mother come back now to rescue her after abandoning her when so small and leaving for Europe? Dreams can be so cruel, setting us up for a fall, terrorising us, rescuing us, then letting us wake to that recurring knowledge of abandonment.

She goes over the day's events, wondering why Marie-Louise behaved so strangely. Perhaps Cowrie is right to be wary of her after all? Yet she spent so many years supporting Rua and working for the anti-nuclear cause after seeing the harm and devastation it caused Maohi families. Maybe it is simply that she is unreliable. Like her own mother. There one minute, gone the next.

She tries to count the stars in the Milky Way, then gradually drifts back into a sound sleep, despite Cowrie snoring loudly beside her.

He pakura ki te po, he kaka ki te ngahere.
A swamp hen in the night, a parrot in the forest.*

Securité
Paris.

"*Madame Verde. C'est le video.*"
"*Merci, Jacques.*"

An elegant woman, dressed in a shimmering green silk suit, takes the video tape from his hand, swivels around in her chair and places it in the VCR. She flicks on the television screen to see footage of her agents boarding and confiscating the *Rainbow Warrior*. The French reporters make it clear that the boats entered French territorial waters illegally and that they are merely acting on government orders. That anyone who trespassed would be treated the same. Then the news flickers back to Bosnia.

Madame Verde is pleased the incident has been given so little coverage. In some countries, they showed footage of the French officers treating the crew roughly. Didn't look good. However, they had their case prepared should that have been shown on French television. It was simply a case of law and order.

The video has rewound to its beginning. Perhaps it's time I moved on, she thinks, as she sets the pause button a moment while she pours out a schnapps. So long a period teaching English to the French, then translating

*Both the parrot and swamp hen mark the passing of time with their cries.

154

for the embassy, becoming an agent and gradually rising through the ranks. She was vital for English-speaking projects with her impeccable accent. Twenty years or so now. Who would have ever thought she'd make it this far? Not those parochial countryfolk back home. She always knew she was cut out for a diplomatic life. But her husband had held her back. No family to worry about now, just endless dinner parties. She sighs, sips her drink and switches the video to Play.

Footage of sand dunes. Amazingly huge sand dunes, the ocean lapping at their feet. She recalls her days in the Sahara, her old life before the French Embassy. The video focuses on a group of women riding bareback over the dunes. She remembers riding bareback in her youth when her father wasn't around. This can't possibly be the right tape. It was supposed to have footage of the military botching an operation and letting those blasted New Zealanders go free. Her task was to see if there was any useful footage that'd make the military look good or show up the amateurism of the protesters, have it transferred to a new video and leaked to the media. She also needs to send footage of the protesters to the video department to blow up. They need to identify who spiked their craft. She reaches for the remote to push Stop when suddenly the tape flicks to the water.

A canoe is being launched. The tape captures it from the water. She takes another sip of schnapps. Beautiful carvings. Then chanting. Nice photography. Another sip. She fast-forwards over the next part until she sees the zodiacs parting company. *Ah, oui.* There's an excellent shot of all the Greenpeace boats within French water. She notes it down. 14.6 minutes into the tape. Then darkness, voices. Fast-forward. Endless black water. Suddenly the camera focuses on a helicopter in the sky. People yelling. Shots. Shots? She'd specifically requested there be no shooting. Bloody fools! More water, yelling, cursing. Zodiac crewed by brown faces. Bound to be Maori activists. Jots it down. 16.7. Probably another one filming. Then suddenly the net flies out of the sky down over them, catching both boats. *Mon Dieu!* These agents couldn't organise a piss-up in a brewery. That's what her English husband used to say.

She laughs. She's never believed in nuclear testing, had marched against the bomb once, but it's her job to oppose the protesters now. Still, only a few months before retirement. Now the French agents are struggling under their own net! What an embarrassment! Thank God the video had got to her before the media. Suddenly the video focuses on a white face in the protest zodiac. Through the netting the face looks familiar. She rewinds the tape and watches it in slow motion. Then she presses the Enlarge button and looks more closely at the face. She hasn't seen her for a while. Only school photographs, then university graduation. She'd been proud that day. Actually thought of making contact, then decided against it. But surely not? She enlarges it still further.

"*Oh, mon Dieu!*" She runs into the ensuite and vomits violently.

..... " the spirit is fearful of the dark " .....

Me te kiore haumiri kakaka.
Like a rat hugging the fence.

News reaches *Manawa Toa* that the Greenpeace boat and her zodiac have been confiscated by the French. There is some dispute over the legality of the operation, since the *Rainbow Warrior* was captured in international waters. But the French, with their unique brand of logic, argue that since the zodiacs are connected to the main boat, then all are guilty. By insinuation, all have entered into French waters. The entire Peace Flotilla is outraged. And so are many governments by now. There is international condemnation of the act and the tide turns in favour of the protesters. France is being isolated, and England with her.

"I say we should ban Pommy goods as well as French. They are in collusion and have also colonised the Pacific," suggests Kuini over breakfast.

Marie-Louise has been burrowed in her research for days now. She looks up. "I think that it's more complex. As much as I detest the use of nuclear force and the military being stationed in Tahiti, I've lived there and know that the Tahitian islands are now dependent upon the French government for housing, education, hospitals, even food."

"Yeah, but that's the very issue. The Maohi people survived before the French arrived and colonisation made them dependent. Who's to say they would not survive again if left to their own devices? Oscar Temaru said the islands are rich in natural resources. Mind you, they'd have to decontaminate some of them now."

"Precisely. It's too late. The Tahitians could not survive without French government support now."

"But surely there's a crucial ethical principle at stake here?" adds Sahara. "The French government has only ever provided services as a bribe for using the islands to test nuclear weapons. If these are to be the last tests, as they say, they'll probably do some gesture of compensation then abandon the contaminated islands to test their weapons by computer. Where does that leave local people?"

"*Oui*, but there's always a choice, *n'est ce pas*?"

"Yeah, like Sophie's choice," states Cowrie. "You have to sacrifice one child for the gas chambers. Which will it be? That's no choice. It's temporary survival but there's still deep pain that can never be healed. All you can do is look after the other child with all your heart."

"What do you mean?" asks Marie-Louise.

"You must see that self-sufficiency and self-determination are crucial to any nation's self-esteem? If one nation takes that off another, let alone raping sacred land by penetrating its surface with nuclear weapons and plugging it with nuclear waste, then even if they finally leave, the woman, the land, is still raped. The trauma lasts a long time. Surely she's better to work her way back to health with her people than constantly being in the company of rapists?"

"You are too emotional about this issue. Colonisation leads to progress. The world has changed. You cannot live a subsistence lifestyle any longer. I realised that when returning to the land with Rua. It's not viable," asserts Marie-Louise. She pours another coffee and retreats into her books.

Cowrie, Kuini, Sahara and Irihapeti wash their dishes and retire to the deck for some air. They discuss the issues, some of which relate to Maori sovereignty also. Sahara asks many questions. She makes links to the situation in Ireland, while acknowledging the vast differences. They admit the issues are complex, cannot be easily solved, but that the crucial fight is to let indigenous people have the chance to rely on their own initiative and resources again.

Cowrie adds it's also a matter of restoring the soul to people. Once this is lost, she says, it's like death. She relates a Hawai'ian story that Paneke told her regarding restoration of the dead. "One of the reasons Paneke is a lomi lomi masseuse is because of its tradition of restoring soul back into body. The corpse is wrapped with fragrant plants to tempt the spirit, and chanting allows it to make the journey back into the body. First you begin with the feet, since the spirit enters the instep or toe, and work your way up. The spirit is fearful of the dark. Finally, there is a purifying bath. After that the body emerges, soul intact, replenished and reinvigorated. The process is called kapuku. During the process, the soul is often depicted as fleeing about the body, over the oceans, over land, visible only to the kahuna who catches it in a gourd and releases it back into the body when it is time."

Kuini responds first. "Kia ora, Cowrie. You offering to massage the soul back into us, then, eh?"

"In your dreams."

"Maybe it'd be more use to Marie-Louise. I'm not sure I trust her."

"Me neither. I didn't like the way she couriered off Sahara's tape without asking her or us. She could have put us all in danger."

"How did she know where to send it?"

"She said she'd copied the address from the notice-board. I never thought to question her further."

"Perhaps we're getting paranoid, but it does seem odd." Cowrie sips her tea and looks out to the ocean. "Maybe we should confront her directly."

"We'd need to be careful. She's been a bit touchy lately. Maybe she just wanted to help. She hasn't had much more than an advisory role on this trip." Kuini, always the mediator, offers to approach her calmly. The others agree. They need to clarify roles so that media releases are appropriately handled.

"It's probably not too late. I can radio in and make sure my colleagues do the editing. They just need to cut out close-ups of us and any identifying information. Black boat, crew in black wetsuits with hoods. I doubt that we'd be in any trouble if it's handled correctly," adds Sahara, preparing to visit the radio room with Iri.

"Let's hope so. Or we might all find ourselves in the hands of the French military like the *Rainbow Warrior* and her crew." Cowrie offers to join Kuini when she confronts Marie-Louise.

161

Ka katokato i te rau pororua.
I am plucking the leaves of the sow-thistles, one by one.

Securité
Paris.

"*Jacques, j'alors au Marseille l'apres-midi pour rendez-vous avec Greenpeace.*"

"*Oui, Madame. C'est ça.*"

Madame Verde, still upset, exits the door of the embassy. She has a crucial decision to make and she knows she needs time away to do it. She'll call from Marseille in the evening and say there have been complications. That she must remain there another week to sort everything out. They know she will not be able to say more over the phone.

Once in her hotel, she extracts the papers, video and a cache of photos and letters she's carried with her over two decades. She had Jacques, whom she could trust, check the identities of those on the video in strict confidence. Interpol verified that the white woman was called Sahara Green, that she'd been arrested several times protesting at Greenham Common. She'd been marked as potentially dangerous since she'd climbed the silos and painted peace symbols on them and also resisted arrest. She remembered hearing about the protest. She was translating for the embassy at the time and never saw the pictures. She'd been on a mission in Germany. The German women were very excited by the bravery of the action and she'd also felt pleased, little knowing her daughter had been involved.

162

Sahara, sweet little Sahara. She remembers holding her in her arms, looking out to the dunes of the Sahara Desert. They'd been happy then. She pours herself a coffee. Tears stream down her face. Her family had disowned her when she became partners with Bill. A working-class miner was their idea of a nightmare as a potential son-in-law. She was cut off from the family wealth and told to fare on her own. She didn't care. They were so happy. Then Bill got posted overseas on a mining contract near the Sahara. She joined him for the happiest months of her life. Sahara, the last of their family, was conceived there. Then the mining company went bust and life became tough. Their relationship began to sour. The only thing that kept her going was the romance of the dunes, the memory of those wild nights exploring a new country, feeling like pioneers in a new land. The vast, mighty Sahara Desert offered new life to them. Reminded her of her childhood holidays on the beaches of France, with their dunes and caves.

She slips the video into the VCR and watches the Hokianga dunes in slow motion. Sahara must be filming, for she only appears once or twice when someone else takes over. She pushes the Hold button, capturing her daughter's face in utter joy as she descends a dune on horseback, heading for the ocean below. She recalls that feeling of joy so well. Although she has fought her way back into respectability, the feeling has long gone. Her risk and adventure are now transferred into being a pawn for the French government. She feels a traitor, to herself, her family, her ideals.

Elizabeth Green sinks to the floor and weeps. She'd cried from time to time, missing them, wondering whether she should make contact, if they'd still love her, yet being too afraid to risk it. But never like this. She weeps decades of hurt, anger and shame. She knew this time would come, had been avoiding facing it for years, throwing herself into her work instead.

At the beginning, becoming an agent was so exciting, recalled that joy of discovery she'd felt with Bill when they met and up to the time Sahara was conceived. That first year with her daughter was idyllic. She'd always wanted a daughter after the three boys. It felt like giving birth to herself when she emerged from the womb. Sahara was a happy child, always full of adventure and inquisitiveness. But once the job ended and Bill was out of work for several years, everything soured. She decided to leave for France to make a new start and return for the children once she was independent. But by then they were settled and happy with Bill, who'd found work at the Ashbourne lime quarries. She made sure she paid for their education and her brother Quentin agreed to accept them at his school. Even Sahara—at a boys' prep school. She'd laughed at that, would have enjoyed it in her youth.

But now her daughter may be in desperate trouble. She fast-forwards and closes in on Sahara beneath the net thrown by her own agents. She, Elizabeth, was responsible for the capture of her daughter. Like a butterfly trapped in a net. The video had cut off after that. She assumed Sahara was on board the *Rainbow Warrior* and the boat was now in custody. If they ever traced Sahara to her, it would put her credibility in danger. She'd lied and said she had no family when applying as a translator. She and Bill had never officially married. They didn't believe in it. The authorities never found out.

But now she's sick of lying and betrayals. She watches the tape over and over, the magic of the dunes, the canoe being lowered into the water, the chanting. Where has her idealism, her beliefs, her spirit gone? She can forgive herself for leaving her family. Times were tough then. The fighting between her and Bill would have hurt them more. But now, she knows she'll never forgive herself if she goes through with the final betrayal of her daughter. There had been talk in the agency of trying to get the protesters arrested and imprisoned on federal offences. After all, they'd tampered with military secrets. They could be indicted and remain in prison for years. The government wanted to discredit the protesters and get the main instigators out of the public eye until the tests were over. Then Chirac would be restored to his "rightful place as a successful president".

But she'd always disliked Chirac since he took power. Petty little man who appeared to have little idea of human nature, ideals, working for a better world. He simply wanted power, like so many others, at the expense of ignoring advice not to conduct the tests and to remove the military from the Pacific. The agency and France had taken a huge knock since the revelation of their involvement in the bombing of the *Rainbow Warrior*. They'd never fully recovered. Many felt they should withdraw from the Pacific and concentrate their energies closer to home. She agreed. But like the Tahitians, she'd become dependent on them for survival. Or has she?

Elizabeth Green mulls over these questions, her life decisions, her huge feeling of loss and grief for two days. She calls Paris and says she needs more time for investigation. She decides it is not too late to act, that she cannot collude in the final betrayal of her daughter for acting just as she herself would have acted if she'd followed her own ideals, not betrayed herself or her family. It's never too late.

At 9 am on the third morning, she enters the video editing studio in Marseille. She has the tape copied for

Sahara. Then the original, tagged by the agency, is edited so it reveals no close-ups but clearly shows the French botch-up. She has the dunes edited out. Then she gets another copy made of the edited tape. She places one edited tape into a courier bag, registers it, and sends it to *Le Monde* with intructions to watch, report and send out to other media. The other goes in a registered courier bag to Paris, with a note explaining she must go to Tahiti to interview the captives. She then places the unedited tape in her handbag and takes a taxi to Air France, where she books a flight to Tahiti.

Me te kiore kai whata.
Like a rat gnawing the food store.

Marie-Louise appears shocked that Kuini could possibly suggest she acted in any way other than for the good of all. She explains she knew it was vital to get the story out because the footage was so powerful. She has no explanation for why they have not yet seen it on television. Perhaps it was intercepted by French authorities? She looks as if she may cry, so Kuini resists hammering her further. Instead, she suggests to Cowrie they leave it another few days then make enquiries. After all, they do not want to attract attention to their exploits and risk their boat being confiscated. Sahara admits that it's possible her colleagues have decided the footage is too risky and are protecting them. She's faxed and the tape has not turned up yet, but it reeks of interference to her.

A few nights after their escapade, another French nuclear explosion is reported. Much larger than the last. Enough to destroy Nagasaki and Hiroshima together. They watch it on screen, exploding the surface of the water, sending chemical waves out toward their boats sitting like night owls who witness at the edge of the watery crater.

With renewed anger, they concentrate on reporting the issues of colonisation and their connection to the nuclear explosions, the effects this has had on the Pacific Islands over the decades. The reports are checked by Kuini and Cowrie and relayed by Irihapeti and Sahara.

167

Sahara is in charge of all couriered material. Marie-Louise does not seem happy about this, argues that her research material is crucial and is aiding the cause, that it must get out on time. They suggest if it is so vital she share the contents with them. This silences her. She says some of the material is too volatile and they have shown themselves to be very emotional over the issues, which of course she understands, but all the same, it must be handled scientifically.

By now, there is definite distrust between them, though she gets on well with some of the men on board, playing quoits and volleyball on the deck. The waiting and watching continue, with high seas whipping the flotilla and revealing their vulnerability in the open ocean.

Excerpts of their mission are shown on global television and they're pleased the footage of the French capturing their own boat and looking stupid is chosen for most of the reports. The media have had a field day and the footage is repeated over and over in all languages. Everyone, it seems, is joyful to see the French agents slip up. They apologise to Marie-Louise for doubting her, but still state that communal action and clear communication are important when working in a team. She agrees. The tension eases, but is not completely gone.

Another week passes. The *Tui* has now left to return to Aotearoa and they will need to sail back to Tahiti to get fresh supplies and petrol soon. Many on board have been violently ill and they are not sure if it is seasickness or contaminated food. They'd been told it was safe to fish from the deck but after the second test, when they saw dead fish floating in the currents, they decided not to risk it. By then, some of the crew had been taken ashore by other flotilla boats returning for supplies.

A meeting is held where they agree they must return to Pape'ete for supplies, and pick up their sick crew and head back to Aotearoa. They reckon they've done all they set out to do, and even if they have not actually stopped the testing as hoped, they've helped attract media attention to the issues and that has resulted in almost universal condemnation of France.

Marie-Louise is jumping ship to return to her family in France for a holiday. Cowrie is not convinced she is trustworthy, though has to admit she was wrong about her. Marie-Louise had sent the video tape on and it had been used.

The final day, they hold a party on board for those left in the Peace Flotilla and there are sad farewells, commitments to further action and a sense of satisfaction that their efforts have not gone in vain, despite the resumption of testing. Chirac has now reduced the tests from eight to six and promises to sign the Pacific anti-nuclear peace treaty and remove the military from Moruroa forever. There are talks of compensation, though all agree that no compensation can rectify the holocaust that testing in the Pacific has created. Its effects will continue for decades, maybe even centuries, as the nuclear waste gradually leaks into the ocean. Already, significant traces of iodine 31, which affects the thyroid gland, strontium 90, which attacks bones, and caesium 137, which works on the cells, have been recorded as far away as South America, Aotearoa and Australia.

The waka has circumnavigated the test zone several times now, attracting media attention. All the Peace Flotilla cheer the crew and everyone joins in the final haka before leaving. Facing Moruroa Atoll, directing their energy to the military, they chant and stomp the deck of *Manawa Toa*. The ancient scow moves with the energy. Their chant surges out over the waves and enters the ocean.

At dawn, they sail toward Pape'ete amidst cheers, dolphins dancing in their bow wake as they slice through these waters a final time. The spirit of Opo has been with them throughout this journey, carved into the prow of the waka and *Manawa Toa*, a harbinger of hope that there is still life in these contaminated waters.

He manga wai koia kia kore e whitikia.
It is a big river indeed that cannot be crossed.

Exhaustion, sadness and elation fill the crew as they sail *Manawa Toa* from Moruroa back to Pape'ete. Memories of their weeks of vigil at the test site coast the shores of their minds. Their morning duties over, Cowrie and Sahara share a cuppa on deck. They recount tales of the trip, noting highlights from their diaries, rereading the mail from home that has helped them through this time by energising their spirits.

"Hey, Cowrie, listen to this. It's a passage from Frederick Cook's diary during his passage over the Antarctic Convergence in his bark *Belgica*, 1898, which Crispin quotes in his letter. It evokes in me the feeling of fear and excitement in the zodiac, skimming the dark water during the eclipse. 'The night which followed was dark', he writes. 'The sea rolled under our stern in huge inky mountains, while the wind scraped the deck with an icy edge. We kept a sharp lookout for icebergs, which might come suddenly into our path out of the impenetrable darkness ahead ... It was a night of uncertainty, of anticipation, of discomfort—an experience which only those who have gone through the wilderness of an unknown sea can understand.' Amazing, huh?"

"That really captures the feeling, Sah. I was shit scared we'd hit a whale or a container. There's nothing more 'unknown' than speeding over a black ocean during an eclipse of the moon."

"Yes! 'The sea rolled under our stern in inky mountains.' I love that bit. This guy was a writer as well as explorer."

"One and the same, Sah, when it's done well. I reckon people write to explore the interior worlds. It's the process of exploration that fires them as much as actually reaching the Pole."

"So, by that account, it isn't just the results of this voyage that are important. It's the journey itself. The fact that we took the risk to protest and believed it'd make a difference?"

"I reckon that's the best way to view it. We should celebrate what we've achieved rather than dwelling on the fact we didn't actually stop them from testing, and use the energy to motivate us and others into further action. Even when the tests end, it's just the beginning for the Maohi to reconstruct their lives without the French, based on their own resources and spirit."

"Do you think the French will relinquish control?"

"Of Moruroa, yes. What do they want with a contaminated island once they can no longer test on it? They're preparing to test by computer now. They'll give the island back, but it won't be the same island they took. It's contaminated, shafted through the middle and plugged with concrete."

"I can't believe the French could ever envisage testing at a site so beautiful. It says a lot about their mindset that they could build such ugly rigs above ground, let alone blast it apart below."

"Yeah—well now you've seen it, you need to keep reporting this, telling the truth of what's happening here in the Pacific to those in the northern hemisphere. It's important you get back home to write while it's still so fresh in your mind."

"It'll never leave my mind, Cowrie. Hey—are you trying to get rid of me?"

"No way. I've felt a deep soul connection with you on this journey. I'd love nothing more than for you to return with me to Te Kotuku. But I need to let go of that. You have vital work to do in Europe—and I need to get that damned novel finished."

"What's the novel about, Cowrie?"

"Its essence is about soul love, acting from heart as well as the head."

"Marie-Louise won't appreciate that book!"

"You're right there. But we don't know. It could touch something in her. After all, her love for Rua moved her out of the French military and into activism."

"And maybe her spots returned again later?"

"They say a leopard never changes its spots. But I believe people can change if they really want to."

"I'd like to believe that. It's why I am a reporter and activist. But sometimes I get bogged down by the sheer weight of the struggles in Europe and the UK."

"Imagine being a small island nation in the Pacific and having to fight colonial powers like France and the USA who are nuking your land, which is your spirit and source of sustenance?"

"Sometimes, I think our gradual disconnection from the land is part of our sense of powerlessness."

"I think you're right, Sah. So what are you going to do to reconnect with the land back home?"

Sahara pauses a moment, realising she is being challenged to do more than write and work from a head place. "My brother Daniel is involved in reforestation in Scotland. I might join him for a while and see what I can learn. Or else join Crispin in Antarctica."

"Great idea, Sah." Cowrie smiles. "We all have the

power to be courageous if we dare. You can tell them about your journey on *Manawa Toa: Heart Warrior*, as inspiration."

Sahara's jade eyes are on fire. She grins as the name of their boat suddenly registers with her. "*Heart Warrior*. I asked a chap on the wharf at Opononi to translate when I saw it being painted onto the boat. He said I'd be told when it was time, that you had to know what it meant from experience."

Cowrie laughs. "He was right then, eh?"

Kuini and Irihapeti join them on deck, and they discuss their future plans. Kuini has ideas for sailing *Manawa Toa* around the Aotearoan coast, taking kids on board for different parts of the journey, so they learn new skills and the history of its voyage. Iri suggests they could take native seeds from the nursery to other marae, beginning with kura kaupapa schools in the north, and Cowrie offers to help. Sahara tells of her plan to become actively involved in reforestation while continuing her media work. As they near Pape'ete, the dolphins leave their bow, having guided them safely to port, and head back to guard Moruroa and Faungataufa atolls.

He peka titoki e kore e whati.
A branch of the titoki tree will not break.

A crowd gathers at Pape'ete pier to greet *Manawa Toa*. Among them, Mauva and Koana, Oscar Temaru and members of Tavini Huraatira, and a group of women's peace activists who'd flown in from Aotearoa to take part in protests and local hui. Among the brown bodies, a tall Englishwoman, her pale face behind dark glasses, stands nervously. Koana thinks she may be a tourist in the wrong place. "Aloha. I'm a foreigner here too. Are you lost?"

The woman appears startled a moment, then replies "No. I'm waiting for the New Zealand boat to return. My daughter is on board."

"You must be proud of her then. They've risked a lot to protest out there."

The woman looks surprised that she is so friendly. "Yes, yes I am proud of her." She pauses. "But it's taken me a long time to realise it."

"That's ok, long as the recognition comes."

"Yes. I think you're right. Thank you." The woman looks as if she needs to be alone, so Koana retreats to the group.

"She's not lost. Her daughter is aboard."

"Is she French or English?" asks Mauva.

"Very British. Upper-crust accent too."

"Can't be Marie-Louise's mother then. Must be Sahara's."

"Na, Cowrie said she hadn't seen her mother for years. That's partly why they bonded so fast. Their real mothers abandoned them at birth or shortly after."

Suddenly *Manawa Toa* comes into view, dolphins at her bowsprit. As the chanting begins, the dolphins leave the boat, heading out to sea. Once she has been tied to the pier, the crew disembark to be greeted by local Maohi with fresh frangipani lei and singing. They respond with a waiata composed by Kuini, telling the tale of their voyage. Their languages are similar enough for the local Maohi to understand most of the song. They are then invited to a farewell feast to be held in their honour that night. A cheer of approval comes from the crew. The crowd gradually disperses.

Standing in the shadow of a container, Elizabeth Green picks out her daughter immediately. One of a few white faces aboard the boat. How grown-up she looks, how confident with these people. Should she re-enter her life now? Is it her right? Has she made a huge mistake by coming? How will she admit her involvement in putting her daughter's life at risk, her betrayal of her family? She stays motionless as Sahara, her arms around her dark friends, begins to walk away. Her feet cannot move.

"Aloha, Koana! I didn't know you were still here!" Cowrie runs toward her cousin, hugging her in joy. She excitedly introduces her to Sahara.

Koana glances over to the woman standing in the shadows. "Do you know that woman, Sahara?"

At that moment, Marie-Louise recognises her boss and moves to greet her. The Englishwoman hands her an air ticket to France and her letter of resignation from the agency. "Please make sure that Jacques gets this," she says. "Don't linger. It's best that you go to the airport as soon as possible." Marie-Louise nods and departs.

Sahara stares at the woman. "I don't think so."

Koana realises she must have made a mistake, that the woman was waiting for Marie-Louise after all. They begin walking up the pier towards the streets of Pape'ete. Just as they move to cross the street to a café, Sahara feels a tap on her shoulder. She turns around.

"Excuse me, but I think this belongs to you." The woman hands her a copy of a video tape marked "For Sahara. With love from Elizabeth Green." Sahara stops, realising who the well-dressed woman is. She tells the others to go on, she'll join them soon. The woman takes off her sunglasses. "Sahara, I am so proud of you today." Tears well in her eyes. "Can you ever forgive me for leaving you? I'd like the chance to explain if possible."

Sahara boils with anger, hurt pride, and rejection spiked with curiosity. She looks into the woman's eyes, trying to remember. Jade eyes, just like hers. And a voice that reminds her of the wind in the dunes. She doesn't know whether she wants to hug her or push her away. Tentatively, she stretches out her hand. "Hello, mother. Your story had better be good." She is proud she can be so strong in front of this woman who has been a myth for most of her life.

"It is painful, but I hope we can get to know each other. It tore me apart to leave you, but I felt I had little choice at the time. Can you spare me some time now?" Sahara glances over to the café where Cowrie is deep in conversation with Koana.

"I'll just tell the others. Wait here." Elizabeth Green watches as her daughter crosses the road, speaks to her friends, who stare back toward her, causing a pang of fear. She wants to escape, yet is torn, desperate to speak to her daughter. She admires Sahara's strong, elegant

177

body, her confidence and spirit as she glides back across the road, recalls her own pioneering spirit at that age.

Sahara says they can have the afternoon together, that she will meet her friends at the feast tonight. They walk to a café further up the road and begin the long journey reclaiming the past, trying to explain, attempting to bridge huge gulfs of misunderstanding. Throughout, Sahara recalls all she has learned on this voyage about listening from the other point of view as well as asserting her own, about the necessity of believing in change, that anyone can change. Eventually they reach the moment Elizabeth has been dreading, the admission that she progressed from interpreter to agent. That she was responsible for attempting to capture her daughter. Sahara is stunned, can hardly believe her ears. She is is so angry she wants to hurl the capuccino into her mother's face.

"Mother, do you realise I could have been strangled in that net? I was so frightened when it came down on us. If Cowrie had not cut me out of it, I might still be there, wound in its tentacles like a fish. Dead."

Elizabeth stiffens, expecting the worst. She does not know how to answer. Tears fill her eyes, tears that have been flowing ever since her decision in Marseille to leave the agency, take the risk to make changes in her life. "I realise I cannot expect forgiveness, Sahara, but I hope that by turning back, facing my mistakes, I can help heal some of the wounds."

Sahara is moved by her honesty, realises this healing is a part of the challenge Cowrie threw to her. Like France, her mother could defiantly defend her decisions. Refuse to listen or to change. But instead she is moving to a new place, taking risks, allowing herself to be vulnerable in the process. This is courageous. Slowly, she reaches over the table to take her mother's hand. "Let's try to understand each other. It may take a while, but I am willing to make the journey if you are."

They remain deep in discussion the next two hours, after which Elizabeth looks at her daughter with pride. "You are worthy of the title of Heart Warrior, Sahara. Wear it proudly."

Tears surge within Sahara. She has waited a lifetime to hear such words from her mother. She never thought she would. She tells her mother some of the bad things she has done so that Elizabeth does not feel alone in her betrayal, of the struggle to grow up with one parent and without a mother present. That she never hated her despite this. That her father had spoken highly of her, had missed her after she left. He'd never taken up with another woman since. Elizabeth is touched by her daughter's honesty, her ability to be present.

"You realise we might never have met again had it not been for your bloody helicopter and that net, and my video camera," admits Sahara.

"Very true. The media did not feature any close-ups of you. I'd never have known unless Marie-Louise had sent us the tape first."

"Marie-Louise? I knew she was a traitor!" Sahara spits out.

"Don't be too hard on her. She did important work for the peace movement. We had a hard time getting her back on board. It was only the bribe of a paid retirement on Le Côte d'Azur that did it in the end, which is more than I'll be getting. I handed her my letter of resignation to take back."

"Truly? You mean you have given up all that for me?"

"For us both. As soon as I saw you riding those mighty dunes down toward the ocean, the joy and freedom in your face, I knew I had to experience that again. And it meant leaving the work I'd fallen into, whether you forgave me later or not."

Sahara is moved. "Mother, would you like to join us for the feast tonight? I know it means crossing to the other side, but you've made the first move already."

"I'd like that very much, Sahara. *Merci beaucoup*."

"I don't think we should tell the others about your role yet though. I'll talk to Cowrie later. I need time to work it through myself, and it'd spoil the end of our trip."

"Mum's the word," smiles Elizabeth.

Sahara grins. They agree to meet at six at the boat. Sahara kisses her on the cheek and goes for a long walk up the shoreline toward Fa'a'a, remembering their last night here, thinking of all that has happened since. A lifetime of experience. And it's not over yet. A part of it is just beginning. Thank you, *Manawa Toa*, for all your lessons. I'll need to draw on your strength to face the future, she thinks, flicking off her sandals and feeling the warm sand beneath her toes.

Ka mahi te tamariki wawahi taha!
Well done, children who break the calabashes!

At Tavini Haraatira Café, Koana and Mauva update the crew on land-based protests. They'd only heard snatches via the radio reports, but it turns out that there's been vigorous debate here in Pape'ete and over all the islands regarding the role of the French. There's stronger support for colonial rule to end, despite the bribes of money for health and education. In response, the crew expand on the events at sea, including the zodiac expedition.

Mauva is shocked. "You mean you polluted our atoll by dumping your zodiac and motor there?" The others realise she is half serious, half teasing them.

Cowrie picks up on her tone. "Don't worry Mauva. With a few more doses of iodine 31, strontium 90 and caesium 137, she'll be a mere skeleton beneath the water."

"When the going gets tough, the tough go tease," adds Koana. They laugh, aware of the brittle edge to their humour.

After hours of tales and laughter and serious talk, Koana and Cowrie walk to the ocean to catch up on family matters. Koana is flying back to Hawai'i in the morning and they will not get another chance alone, with the feast tonight.

She tells Cowrie that she and Mauva are lovers, which Cowrie intuited from their closeness. They are both committed to their own sovereignty movements, which means they meet often at indigenous Pacific conferences,

181

but each has decided to live on her own islands to work for her people.

"Sounds like the decision Peta and I had to make," offers Cowrie.

"Yes. It's not easy, but we are happiest doing the work we believe in."

"I understand that Ko. She's gorgeous. I'm rapt for you."

"So, are you and Sahara lovers?"

"No. I wondered at one point. But it turns out that she's heterosexual."

"So was I. Remember, Cowrie?"

"How could I forget, Ko?" Cowrie laughs. "But this time it feels ok. We understand each other across our different cultures, and she has an amazing ability to be intimate. She loves talkstory and she's open to new ideas. I adore her enthusiasm. She knows how to follow her intuition and she's destroying some of my prejudices against the Poms!"

"Now that last bit sounds serious, Cowrie. Be careful!"

They walk toward the rocks at the far end of the beach. "Weird about Sahara's mother turning up, don't you think?" says Koana.

"Sure is. I know she hasn't seen her since she was a small child. What a journey this has been for her, eh?"

"Sure. Did it make you feel sad?"

"How?"

"Like, still not having met your own birth mother."

"No. Not really. I do wonder, but I've had a good life with Mere. I might be disappointed if my birth mother ever turned up. She might not be what I imagined."

"Bet it's a real shock for Sahara then. She's gonna need your support tonight, Cowrie."

"She's got it. I hope she's ok. It's not going to be easy for her."

They sit on edge of the rocks, dangling their feet in the water, talking about friends and family, life back in Aotearoa and Hawai'i, catching up on gossip. Eventually, Sahara appears up the other end of the beach, heading toward the boat. "I'd better go and see if she's ok, Ko. See you tonight at the feast."

"Sure thing, Cowrie. Malama pono."

"Kia ora, Ko."

They depart with a hug. Cowrie follows Sahara aboard *Manawa Toa*.

He toa taumata rau.
Bravery has many resting places.

"You ok, Sah, or do you want time alone?" Cowrie asks, once she's caught up with her friend on the deck.

"I've spent the last hour on my own, pacing the beach, trying to make sense of it all. I must admit, I'm still confused."

"Wanna share it?"

"Thanks."

They settle under their hammocks, where they'd talked in peace on the voyage, and Sahara spills out everything. All, that is, except her mother's role as an agent. Cowrie listens carefully, is astonished, but senses that something is still missing from the tale, that Sahara will tell her in time. Just the trauma of meeting her mother again is enough to handle. She notices the video in her bag. "So what's this? Baby shots of little Sah?" Cowrie teases her.

She reads the message. For Sahara. With love from Elizabeth Green.

"No. It's a copy of the video of our trip."

"Where did she come across it? Does she work for the media?"

Sahara is about to say yes when she bursts into tears. Cowrie holds her, rocking her. "Hey Sah. Sorry I teased you. It's been a big day. Just tell me what feels right."

That is all Sahara needs. She knows she cannot go on protecting her mother, nor does she want to get into the

184

pattern of telling lies. Yet she fears Cowrie will be angry, hate her mother and reject her also. She tells her this.

"What can be so bad, Sah? She looked like a very nice woman. For a Pom, that is." Cowrie tries to lighten the mood.

"That's what I'm afraid of, Cowrie. What's the very worst you could imagine? What if you found out your own mother worked for the enemy?"

"I dunno, Sah. My own birth mother might, for all I know."

Sahara is silent a moment. "I'm serious, Cowrie. Tell me the very worst that could happen."

"Well," says Cowrie, trying to think of the most ludicrous situation possible, "I guess it could be worse. At least your mother's English. Imagine if you found out she was a French agent? Now that'd be the pits."

Sahara bursts into tears again and Cowrie consoles her, wondering what could have set her off again. Maybe her mother is a criminal or has a terrible past to hide? "Hey Sah, I promise not to be angry or make fun, no matter how bad or evil or terrible your mother has been."

"Cross your heart and hope to die?"

"I'd never cross my heart or hope to die—but you have it on my word of honour."

"Well, you're right. She left England, was cut off from her inheritance when she had children with Bill and ended up working as a translator in France."

"Is that all?"

"Listen, Cowrie."

"Ok. All ears."

"She got work translating for French Securité. They were so impressed with her skills, they eventually made her an agent. She'd always loved adventure, but hadn't banked on the price she'd pay for neglecting her own ideals. She'd been thinking of leaving, but seeing me on the video, it all came together in her mind and she resigned. Her first act of reconciliation for her new life was to meet me again and try to make a new start."

Cowrie is speechless. Sahara waits anxiously for her reply. After a long silence, Cowrie sighs. "She made a huge mistake and I should feel bloody angry, but the reality is that if it wasn't her in that role it'd have been someone else. The important part is that she had the courage to realise her mistake and begin to make amends. Besides, with her knowledge, she'd be invaluable to the peace movement, so there's some hope for change here, Sah. After all, the founder of Greenpeace was once a successful industrialist. I know heaps of people who've seen the light and altered their ways. They are often the most motivated activists."

Sahara hugs her, not wanting to let go. "Thank you, Cowrie. If you can forgive Elizabeth, then maybe I can too."

"Well, only if she spills all," jokes Cowrie. "I'll be there with my notebook."

"I invited her to the feast tonight. But I can call her at the hotel if you think it'd be wrong for her to be there. I just wasn't sure what to do. I want her to see my friends, see the power of this movement, see the other side of things."

Cowrie creases her brow and thinks a moment, then replies. "I agree. She'll have to listen to many speeches about the effects of her actions from those who've suffered. It won't be easy for her. But it'll be a good starting point."

"You know, you are very subversive suggesting she use her knowledge to help get rid of colonisation here. I'd never have thought of that."

"Cunning as a kiore," responds Cowrie. "You learn to use all resources and to network when you're opposing such vast power systems. Sah, I'm going to ask you a difficult question now. Are you absolutely sure we can trust her?"

"Yes. I've thought about that all afternoon. She began with the kinds of ideals we share. I know that from Dad's words too—and uncle Quentin talked about their days growing up as if she were an activist way back then. She's handed in her resignation at the agency but it may take some time before she's ready to commit herself to new action. She's asked me to fly back to Britain and stay with her a few weeks while I recover from the trip and so we can get to know each other better. I said I'd tell her tonight. But I think I will. Then I can really suss out if she'd help and let you know."

"Great. Subversive future plans. I like it, Sah. I'll go put on a cuppa while you pack if you're leaving tomorrow."

In the galley, Cowrie cries, knowing how much she'll miss her friend, wondering what it would be like to be in her situation. She cannot believe that Sahara's mother could have been partly responsible for nearly capturing them. It's so bizarre it's almost funny. Mind you, if her knowledge could be harnessed, she could be very valuable. Then she has an idea. She picks up her kete, already falling apart at the edges from too much time in salt water. She empties it and cuts a square from the woven flax. She then separates the strands and makes a card from the corner of a Weetbix box, writing on it with an indelible marker. Proud of her handiwork, she wraps it in greaseproof paper and places it in her pocket, then begins to prepare for their last night on Maohi soil.

Kaore e pau, he ika unahi nui.
A fish covered with large scales will never be eaten.

The farewell feast is delicious and the speeches moving. Bonds have been created during this time of struggle that will be lasting. There is acknowledgment that the nuclear tests have not been stopped, but the protests have been successful in attracting international condemnation and the remaining tests have been reduced from eight to six. That is cause for celebration. The end is in sight.

A former military worker tells them that France is second only to the USA in the number of military installations it has outside its own land, that after the tests are over, they must keep fighting to make sure they rid their shores of the military forever. Moruroa and Fangataufa atolls must be returned to Maohi people as clean as they can be made, with all traces of nuclear waste and military buildings gone. That they must keep up the pressure of world attention and make sure this is done. "We must insist they leave our islands so we can resume a sustainable existence." That brings cheers from the crowd.

During the proceedings, Cowrie keeps a close eye on Elizabeth Green, trying to gauge her responses. Sahara had introduced her before the speeches and they'd talked about their love of the dunes. She reckoned that was a safe topic for now. At one point in the speeches, Elizabeth whispers to her daughter and Sahara passes on to Cowrie that the fella holding the video is actually a

French agent. Cowrie asks Mauva who he is. She says he's been at all their marches. Cowrie replies she has it on good authority that he's a French agent. Mauva approaches and asks him outright. He denies it, but disappears as soon as she turns her back. Elizabeth smirks with satisfaction. Cowrie is sure she'll jump ship and join them eventually. She likes something about this woman. She has Sahara's jade eyes, her sense of courage and determination.

After the speeches, they settle down to a wonderful feast. Cowrie sits opposite Sahara and her mother. Towards the end of the night, she hands over her parcel surreptitiously to Elizabeth. Sahara leans over as her mother unravels the greaseproof paper to reveal a square of basket. Her brow creases in bemusement. Then she reads the note: "*Ka pu te ruha ka hao te rangatahi*: The old net lies in a heap while the new net goes fishing.— From the one who got away!" Both Sahara and her mother realise the woven mat represents the net sent showering down on them from the French helicopter and this is Cowrie's way of getting utu while also acknowledging Elizabeth. Letting her know she knows. They look at each other in amazement, then burst out laughing.

"Touché, Cowrie," smiles Elizabeth. "A woman after my own heart!"

"Well, after your daughter's, actually, but where there's a will, there's a way."

"Where there's a net, Cowrie will be fishing," Sahara adds, her eyes glinting in amazement at her audacity, loving her for having the audacity to do this.

The feast ends with fresh fruit—melons, pawpaw, mangoes and coconuts, which, Mauva insists, come from the outer islands and are relatively safe. They risk it for tonight, feasting and singing until late. Sahara's mother leaves after the speeches and dinner, arranging to meet her daughter in the morning, and making sure she gives Cowrie a special farewell hug. "Thank you for looking after Sahara so well, Cowrie. I owe you."

"I have ideas on how to make the repayment, Elizabeth, but I'll let Sahara tell you later. By the way, thanks for alerting us to the outsider."

"No problem. There's more information where that came from."

"You read me well, Elizabeth. I'm sure we'll meet in the future."

"I look forward to it. Thanks again."

"*Merci beaucoup*," replies Cowrie. Elizabeth grins, thinking that this Cowrie would make an excellent agent herself, and walks away after kissing her daughter farewell.

That night, Cowrie and Sahara cuddle together in one hammock. They look up into the night sky and Sahara picks out the Southern Cross flying her kite on a different angle from Aotearoa, her tail spraying stars back into the Milky Way.

"Hey, what's that one Cowrie? With the arrow?"

"That," replies Cowrie, "is a Heart Warrior. You can see her in the northern hemisphere. It'll remind you of who you are and of this voyage. *Me te mea ko Kopu ka rere i te pae*: like the star Venus as she rises above the horizon …"

"And you," whispers Sahara, a tear in the corner of her eye, as she snuggles into Cowrie's arms for their last sweet night together.

Above them, the sky sparkles stars that guided the first Pacific navigators to these islands and will continue long after nuclear explosions have left. Below, a lone dolphin rests in the dark waters, preparing to guide the Heart Warrior safely home to Aotearoa. *Haere e whai i te waewae o Uenuku, kia ora ai te tangata.* Good fortune comes to those with the memory of going to the feet of Uenuku.

Glossary

See *Cowrie* and *The Journey Home* for further glossaries. All words are Maori, colloquial New Zealand English, Hawai'ian [H], or Samoan [S].

ae: yes.
ahi: tuna fish [H].
akiaki: red-billed seagull.
aloha: greeting, also love, in Hawai'i.
Aotearoa: Northland, New Zealand.
aroha: love.
beadies: beady eyes.
bickie jar: jar of biscuits.
bush telegraph: informal communication network.
cuzzies: cousins.
dak: dope, marijuana. Colonial rule has made this often the only source of income for dispossessed islanders, as in many Third World countries.
e oma! let's go! come on!
feijoa: native fruit, of guava family.
goer, as in "she's a goer": she is ok, she gets involved, moves, goes.
Great Turtle Island: Native American name for USA.
haka: dance of challenge.
hangi: underground cooking.
haole: white person [H].
Hau Atoll: Pacific atoll where French agents who bombed the Greenpeace *Rainbow Warrior* in Auckland Harbour were sent as "punishment" by the French government, who had ordered the bombing. Both agents were let free before their sentences were served. A Greenpeace photographer was killed when the boat was bombed and others nearly missed being exploded but escaped the boat in time.
hei matau: bone fishhook.

heiau: temple, sacred stone building [H].

hoea: paddle; also used for spear because paddle is in shape of a spear.

huhu: large bug.

hui: meeting.

hula: Hawai'ian dance.

ieie: vine that curls around walls and trees like octopus tentacles [H].

ika: fish.

iwi: tribe.

kahawai: fish.

kahuna: Hawai'ian priest or elder.

kai: food.

kai moana: seafood.

kamaha'o: wonderful [H].

Kanaka Maoli: Hawai'ian Independence Movement [H].

ka pai: go well, all's well.

kapuku: process of soul travelling from body (see text for context) [H].

karakia: prayer.

kava: Fijian liquor.

kete: woven kit or bag, usually made from flax.

kia kaha: stay strong.

kia ora: hullo, greetings; also used as expression of agreement.

kihini: kitchen.

kina: sea egg.

kiore: Polynesian rat.

kohanga reo: lit. language nest. Preschool programmes conducted in Maori.

korero: talk, speech.

koru: spiral design with spiritual signifiance, like a fern frond in shape.

kuia: wise woman elder.

kumara: Maori sweet potato.

kupua: elders [H].

kura kaupapa: Maori-language immersion secondary schools.

lavalava: pareu or cloth worn around body [S].

lehua: blossom of o'hia tree, large sprawling tree like the pohutukawa tree in Aotearoa. with exquisite red or yellow blossom in summer [H].

lei: neck garland of flowers [H].

mahalo: thank you [H].

malama pono: much love [H].

manu toetoe: kite made from pampas grass.

Manawa Toa: Heart Warrior.

manuka: tea tree.

marae: gathering place for Maori.

mere: club.

MMP: Mixed Member Proportional Representation (form of government in Aotearoa).

mokopuna: grandchildren.

Nga Puhi: Northland tribe to which Cowrie belongs.

Ngati Cyberspace: Ngati is used for tribe—so hence here, cyberspace internet tribe.

nikau: native palm tree of Aotearoa.

Opononi: Home of Opo, the gay dolphin, in the Hokianga Harbour, Tai Tokerau.

pakeha: white person.

Papatuanuku: Earth Mother, earth we live on, Aotearoa.

paua: black shellfish with bright green-blue shells, like abalone.

pohutukawa: native tree which blooms in summer.

poi: liquid made from beaten taro plant [H].

pounamu: greenstone, native jade found in Aotearoa.

powhiri: welcome.

pukapuka: book.

rellies: relatives.

rubber ducks: inflatable boats (widely used in Aotearoa).

ruru: owl.

squizzy, as in "have a squizzy": have a look.

suss out: investigate.

Tai Tokerau: Northland, Aotearoa.

takapu: gannet.

tangata whenua: people of the land.

taninha: monster.

taonga: sacred gift.

tapa: beaten cloth, usually decorated with berry dyes.

Te Aroha: name of Kuini's sexual abuse programme; "aroha" lit. means "love".

Te Kotuku: Te Kotuku Marae, named after the kotuku or rare white heron.

toetoe: pampas grass.

torea: oystercatcher (bird).

tuatua: shellfish.

Uenuku: God of the Rainbow, he passed on wisdom to those who were willing to hear.

utu: revenge.

wahine: woman.

waiata: song.

waka: Maori canoe; also used in text for modern canoe or kayak.

weta: large insect like a huge cricket, with barbed legs and awesome jaws.

whakamutu! be quiet!

whanau: family.

whare nui: large house, meeting house, as the marae.

wheke: octopus.

Also by Cathie Dunsford

Cowrie
Cathie Dunsford
Cath Dunsford's first novel (of a series I hope) is a gentle determined, insightful and womanful book.

Keri Hulme

Cowrie is tightly woven, texted with colors, tastes and smells ... and definitely worth the read, so go bug your local bookstore.

Fat Girl Magazine

ISBN 1-875559-28-0

The Journey Home: Te Haerenga Kainga
Cathie Dunsford
This is lesbian fantasy dripping with luscious erotic imagery.

NZ Herald

ISBN 1-875559-54-X

If you would like to know more about Spinifex Press write for a free catalogue or visit our website

Spinifex Press
PO Box 212 North Melbourne
Victoria 3051 Australia
<http://www.spinifexpress.com.au>